AMAZING
GRACE NEWTON
and THE RV TRIP

AMAZING
GRACE NEWTON
and THE RV TRIP

N. JANE QUACKENBUSH

For information regarding permission, write to:
Attention: Hidden Wolf Books
155 West Genung St., St. Augustine, FL 32086

Copyright © 2018 by N. Jane Quackenbush
All rights reserved.
Published in the United States by Hidden Wolf Books.

ISBN 9780999434567
Library of Congress Control Number: 2018949970

Text set in Adobe Garamond

Version 1.1
Printed in the United States of America
First edition paperback printed, September 2018

d

To my family and friends.

Special thanks to
Kika Iadanza for her laser beams,
Joan Pospichal-LeBoss for rereading,
and my beautiful mother for her everything.

To: Clara

Stay Amazing!

N & Jan Quill

৩৯ *One* ৫৬

Let's Go

It was barely dawn when Aunt Esther quietly padded into my bedroom. I was afraid the time for her to leave would come before I was ready. I didn't want to say goodbye.

"Are you leaving?" I sleepily asked.

"I am, yes, very soon."

My face turned upside down. "No, I don't want you to go," I softly pleaded as I rolled around in my sheets.

"Well, Grace, how would you like to come along with us this time?" she asked.

My eyes shot open!

Tossing away the covers, I sat up in a dither. All my life, I had always wanted to go camping, or RVing, or whatever you called it. "Could I?"

"If you want to?"

"Yes! I want to. Is everyone else coming, too?"

"I think it's just going to be you kids, Alice, and me."

"Not Momma and Papa?"

"I think they could use some alone time, don't you?"

After a few moments of thought, I said, "Yeah, they could."

Aunt Esther patted my leg and said, "Well, if we're going to get going, we gotta get going!"

I threw off the rest of my covers and started to get ready. "I'll be ready in a flash!"

I packed all the essentials like socks, rollerblades, safety gear, butterfly wings, Noodle, and his green-screened travel kit. He would love going on the road! I almost forgot some travel clothes for Noodle … He wouldn't want to travel naked! After I had everything packed in my purple polka dot roly-suitcase, I ambled down the stairs where everyone was eating a hearty, sweet-smelling breakfast.

"I'm ready!" I cheerfully stated.

"All packed?" Momma asked.

"Uh-huh!" I assured her.

Hope had a doubtful expression on her face. "I bet you didn't pack any underwear, did you?" she asked, but it sounded more like a statement. My expression must have said more than my mouth because Hope was right. "Grace! Did you remember to pack any shirts, shorts, bathing suits, or socks?"

"Oh, yes!" I said excitedly. "Socks! I did pack socks! I need them for when I'm rollerblading."

"Oh my stars! Grace, you need more than socks and rollerblades, *for crying out loud*!" Hope sounded more like my mother than my older sister sometimes. "Let's see what you have in here …"

Hope unzipped my suitcase and out popped all my necessaries. I ran upstairs to get Noodle so Hope could see how I had remembered to take him along, too.

"You aren't really going to bring *that*, are you?" Hope gave Noodle a disgusted look. I felt bad that Hope was possibly hurting Noodle's tender feelings. I looked at my little nugget as he blissfully pecked at nothing.

Abel zoomed past with his speedy little legs and his new handmade superhero cape unfurling behind him. He flew up the stairs without a word. I could hear a bunch of thumping and clanking in his room before he came down and showed Hope *his* suitcase for her to inspect.

"Nice job, Abel! You even packed your toothbrush and toothpaste." Hope sounded so surprised with his thoughtfulness. She gave me a look that said, *See, even a little boy is smarter than you.* Abel smiled proudly with his chest puffed out and hands at his waist.

"Wow, Abel, you did such a good job!" Aunt Esther said.

"I'm very proud of you, son," Papa said while Momma looked on and smiled.

Aunt Esther's traveling friend, Alice, came in from outside and said, "Ol' Tex is ready for passengers if you're all ready and packed."

Hope and Abel turned to her and quickly scrambled out the door with their baggage. I felt a little silly with my kid brother being a better packer than I, so I went back upstairs and pretty much repacked my whole situation … this time with the "real" essentials and a couple of bonus items. I came back down sure that I was not forgetting a thing.

I grabbed Noodle to bring him along, but Momma said that it might not be the best idea to bring my pet chicken camping.

"But who's going to take care of him when I'm gone?"

"Your father and I will make sure that Noodle is fed and extra happy."

"And dressed," Papa said with a wink.

Papa made me blush.

"I just don't want Noodle to get lost, okay?" Momma said.

Momma was right. Noodle could get lost, and then I might never find him.

"Okay," I said sadly, knowing she was right.

I stuffed a couple of pancakes into my mouth and packed away some bacon and sausage just in case I got hungry later. I gulped down a big glass of apple juice and confidently boarded Ol' Tex without my little, not-so-yellow Noodle ... but he'd be safer here ... at home ... I hoped.

AND THE RV TRIP

ҩ *Two* ҩ

Goodbyes

It looked like Hope, Abel, and I were sharing the bunk beds—meaning Hope would take the bottom bunk while Abel and I would sleep on the top. Abel and I each took the opposite ends to place our pillows. Aunt Esther slept in the overhead bed above the driver's seat, and Alice had the couch that turned into a bed.

Abel and I put our face prints on the

windows as we peered out with smiles and visions of our upcoming adventure that awaited. Everything looked so different from inside the RV. Our house looked so cozy—like a place I would like to visit if I didn't already live there.

We lived in a treehouse, a real, honest to goodness treehouse. I told you this before, but sometimes people don't believe me when I tell them about our living accommodations. Behind the broad front porch that looked so inviting stood the strong, wide, tall trunk with windows that traveled up two stories, leading to vines covered in colorful flowers that overflowed in every direction. Oh, I can't forget, the white paint on the additions were accented with pale green shutters. (Momma insisted on pale green shutters.)

Momma stood behind the opened top of the Dutch door holding Noodle in his travel cage while Papa slid his arms around Momma's waist. She didn't pull away; she rested her head against his strong shoulders.

Momma was a lot more peaceful this morning. She didn't have the same sadness in her eyes as she had the days and weeks before.

She was still quiet, but that was typical. It was a good start, I thought.

Abel was arranging his action figures along the rails which made me think that I should probably get to decorating my side of the bed, too. I put my softest, colorful, comfy, fluffy blankets on top of the striped sheets that were already there. My favorite stuffed bunny, Lumps, rested on my pillow until nighttime.

After Aunt Esther and Alice finished putting all of our food and provisions away, checked everything over once, and then again … it was finally time to go. I couldn't wait to depart. It was almost 11:00 o'clock *and* we had been talking about leaving since 7:00 AM, *for crying out loud*!

I looked over to my twinkling apple tree and saw a sparkle dance across the purple puddle. I almost forgot to say goodbye to Mazie!

"Wait! I forgot something. I'll be right back," I yelled to everyone, but no one seemed to be paying any attention anyway. I jumped off of the RV steps and waddled over to the puddle.

Mazie smiled at me.

"Mazie, I'll be back soon. We're going on an RV trip with Aunt Esther, Alice, Hope, and Abel in Ol' Tex."

"That sounds super fun!" she said happily. I was going to miss Mazie. I liked seeing her every day. As if she could read my thoughts, she said, "I'll be right here when you return."

"Promise?"

"Promise."

AND THE RV TRIP

ᔕᓂ *Three* ᓍᔕ

Over The River

Momma and Papa came out of the treehouse to give each of us careful, last-minute instructions on not fighting, being good, as well as listening to Aunt Esther and Alice.

"Yes, ma'am, yes, sir," we promised. After a couple rounds of big, sloppy kisses, we were finally set to leave.

Ol' Tex sputtered as Aunt Esther turned the ignition.

"C'mon, Texi!" Aunt Esther pumped the gas pedal, then the RV roared to a start before quieting to a gentle hum. "Thatta guy!" Aunt Esther smiled. I could see her grinning mouth in the rearview mirror.

"Where are we headed?" Hope asked.

"Over the river and through the woods to places we ought to go!" Aunt Esther sang.

"No, for real?" Hope always needed to know everything at all times.

"How about this, you'll know when we get there."

Hope's face split into disappointment mixed with mostly concern. She didn't like not knowing everything. As we drove down the hill, I looked back toward our flowering, towering treehouse. Momma and Papa waved to us from the porch. I waved back, wondering if I would miss them too much.

Momma had sent us off with a variety of apple baked goods. I sure was grateful for all of our apples. When we got near Nana's cottage, I pictured her standing on her wooden porch waving to us as we set off on our journey.

Nana's dance party celebration last night was way better than that boring funeral that was held a few weeks back. My feet had so many blisters from all the dancing that I wasn't sure if I would be able to rollerblade for a couple of days. I knew Nana was happy in the afterlife looking down at us from Heaven having a good ol' time in her "boogie barn" as it was known to Apple Valley locals.

We stopped at the bottom of our winding ridge, took a left, then headed to who knows where.

The rolling hills danced beside us as Aunt Esther turned up the tunes. By the second verse, we were all singing along with The Carpenters, my momma's favorite band.

"I'm at the top of the world looking down on creation
and the only explanation I can find,
is love I have found ever since you've been around …"

The songs enhanced the overall excitement that went along with our expedition. We sang all the way to our exciting first stop—the gas station. Ol' Tex was a thirsty RV because he guzzled what Aunt Esther said seemed to be a thousand gallons of gas an hour.

At the gas station, Hope, Abel, and I took turns going to the dirty, grimy bathroom. I tried to not touch anything after washing my hands. Unfortunately, I would be stuck inside the bathroom if I didn't pull on the handle.

When I came out, Hope and Abel were looking at a case filled with donuts. Suddenly my mouth watered. Thankfully, Aunt Esther had gathered a bunch of junk food for us to munch on as we motored along the highway, happily stuffing our faces.

As we drove westward, I watched the colors in the sky turn from baby blue to orange popsicle to dark purple velvet. The bright headlights hypnotically blinked between the trees while the red tail lights stayed steady, ahead on the open road.

"Think it's time for a game of checkers, or what?" Alice said.

"Huh?" I quickly came out of my stupor. "Oh, yeah, let's play!"

Alice got out the game; then she and I squared off while Hope and Abel battled for chips.

I started off feeling pretty confident in my moves. They weren't super but not too shabby either. So far, I still had all of my chips … that was before we finally faced off. Needless to say, Alice beat me horribly, fair and square.

I asked her to let me win (*after she didn't seem to understand my silent hint*) but she said to me, "You wouldn't really be winning if I let you win, right?"

"Um …"

"You see those medals behind you?" Alice pointed.

I turned to see two big, shiny gold medals and one silver one, hanging from thick, red, white, and blue ribbons. "Yes."

"I had to earn those silver medals in the 1984 and 1988 Olympics. The other gold one I won at the world championships."

"Oh," I said, impressed.

"Guess what?"

"What?"

"No one *let* me win those. I had to work extremely hard, train even harder, and outsmart my opponents in order win them."

Alice was an Olympian? I was stunned.

I hadn't noticed her athletic build until now. Before I knew that she was a real live superwoman, all I noticed was her wide, bright smile and warm, welcoming eyes against her flawless, bronze skin.

"Do you understand what I'm saying?" she asked while examining my features.

I'll admit, I was a tad confused, but after I thought about *earning* your reward versus being given a token prize, I understood.

"Yes," I said.

I was ready to play to win, fair and square. I only wanted to win if I actually earned it. Needless to say, after countless losing matches, my eyes struggled to stay open. Apparently, Alice was super competitive on and off the track.

"Grace, you wanna join Abel in going to sleep?" Alice asked.

I looked up from the game and noticed that Hope and Abel weren't playing checkers anymore. I looked back to the bunk beds and saw them both snoozing as if they had been there a while.

"Oh, yeah. I guess so," I yawned as I got up

to walk back to my bunk. My teeth felt fuzzy so I brushed them before climbing up to my bed. I pulled my fluffy blanket up to my chin then turned over to face the window as we traveled along the road. My eyes fought to keep up with the passing trees.

My body barely moved as it traveled along a dark forested highway to who knows where.

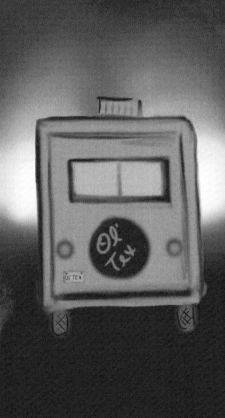

৵ *Four* ৶
Through The Woods

Blueness caused the darkness to fade away from behind my closed eyes. I opened my lids slowly then closed them back quickly. I knew that I had seen daylight but I wasn't ready for it. We were not moving; I knew that much. The daylight and stillness must have taken me away from my rest. Or maybe it was the sound of Abel running around outside screeching like some sort of wild animal.

"Grace, are you awake?" Aunt Esther asked.

"Huh?" I turned over to see her smiling face greeting me. "Yes, are we there?" I sleepily asked.

"Where?"

"Over the river and through the woods?" I slowly sang in my scratchy morning voice.

"Yes, we are definitely through the woods. In fact, we are going to go into the belly of the earth!" she said with her eyes widening.

"The belly of the earth? Will it eat us?" I asked.

"Only if you're extra yummy!" she said as she tickled my belly.

I giggled, rolling around until I climbed down from my bunk.

Aunt Esther had placed an oval-shaped pastry on the table, topped with white icing. It looked interesting.

"Want some Danish Puff?" she asked.

"What's Danish Puff?" (Recipe in back)

"If you've never had Danish Puff, then you've not experienced bliss!" Aunt Esther said as she was cutting off a long rectangular slice.

I sniffed the pastry and found the scent

most certainly acceptable. But the taste was out-of-this-world delicious! There were layers of softness wrapped with a sweet shell and topped with an icing that had a flavor that sent you to instant bliss. Aunt Esther was right!

Along with the Danish Puff, I ate some granola, yogurt, and chased it all down with some milk. Guess I was having too much fun at breakfast to notice that Hope and Abel were outside playing catch with Alice. Alice could toss the football like Papa, but it seemed to float down gently into Hope and Abel's grip.

There wasn't a boink sound; it was more of a thunk sound. It had me thinking … I could probably catch *her* footballs without blistering my palms or breaking a finger. … *hmmmm* … They looked like they were having a whole lot of fun, and I wanted in on the action.

I quickly scarfed down my breakfast, ran outside, and signaled for Alice to toss me the ball. Alice stopped mid toss toward Abel then redirected her throw to me. As it was suspended in the air, I had a flashback to the painful lofts my papa had thrown and considered letting the ball bounce recklessly to the ground. But I saw a boy getting out of his car in the parking lot, watching as the ball traveled in the air toward me … I resolved to not look like a girl.

I held out my hands as the oblong stinger dropped painlessly into my awaiting grip. Suddenly the fear I had of a football possibly hurting my hands disappeared, and I launched a sweet arching toss over to Abel who was so mesmerized by my awesome catch that he fumbled the ball.

"Ha ha!" I rubbed it in. Yes, of course, it was a solo celebration, my football catching that is, but that was okay. Plus, the boy I was trying to impress wasn't even looking anymore. But what had me excited was that, I was able to let a stupid fear go. It was gone, and I would never let another football scare me again—I hoped. All was good as we continued tossing the football back and forth.

"You guys ready?" Aunt Esther asked as she signaled for us to actually pay attention to where we were.

I looked over to the red metal building that read "**Tuckaleechee Caverns**: Greatest site under the Smokies".

We walked into the musty, brown carpeted room where they sold fudge and admission tickets to the right. To the left was a whole room filled with t-shirts, hats, snow globes, books, coon-tail hats, bubblegum, and other trinkets. The candy and fudge tried very hard but couldn't quite mask the underlying smell of mildew.

I perused around the colorful goodies wishing I had tons of money to give to the cigarette smoking sales clerk in exchange for these fine treasures that would remind me of our barely begun travels that I already knew I would never forget.

∽ • ∽

"Y'all rascals ready to be swallered up by the belly of the earth?" the ticket salesman asked. He had a long straggly beard, snaggly teeth, and leathery skin like our football, only a lot more crinkled. Abel and I hid behind Aunt Esther when the "caveman" set his wild eyes on us.

"It's okay, kids. He won't hurt cha," Alice promised.

The man lifted his long knobby index finger then said, "I'm not hungry right chet, but I'll tell ya, Cavie over yonder likes swallerin' lil' youngins such as those two near every day," he winked at Abel and me as he pointed to the cave entry then let out a heinous cackle that sent chills down my spine.

I looked to where he had pointed. Was that the belly of the earth? It didn't look like a belly. It looked like a ramshackle archway that led to an uninteresting hall.

"Calling all cave explorers … calling all cave explorers. Your tour is about to begin," I heard an unenthusiastic woman announce. Aunt Esther and everyone else were already standing in front of the short-haired lady, ready to go on the tour. I hurried over after giving the old hillbilly one last glance. As he smiled, his teeth moved back and forth like piano keys playing a tune.

"Hey, I'm Rocky and I'll be your cave guide today. Stay close and don't wander off alone, specially, you youngins'," the tomboyish lady said as she gave Abel and I a careful look. She mumbled a few more words that the adults seemed to listen to, but all I could do was look around.

Slowly, we descended an aluminum ramp and then made our way into "the belly". A long, steep, dark, narrow set of rickety stairs waited for us to carefully step down. When we came to a landing, I scanned the earthen cavity. It looked empty, so it must have been hungry.

As we came to a steeper set of stairs, it appeared that we were about to be swallowed whole in one gulp. I became fearful, thinking about what that old, bearded man had said earlier. But when I saw the same boy who I had hoped witnessed my perfect football catch looking so relaxed, I decided to be brave for him. I didn't want him to think I was a nincompoop. So I put on my brave face and pretended that walking down a super steep set of tiny metal steps was not a big deal.

The deeper we went, the more I could hear water trickling. When I tuned into the guide, she explained that a fresh water river flowed throughout the cavern. Colored lights illuminated the formations that were made thousands of years ago by endless changes in the flow of waters.

This was a magical place. I almost couldn't believe it myself ... It looked like a dark rainbow-colored fantasyland—all underground! I forgot about the scary hillbilly. All I could do was stare in awe at the marvelous beauty. We saw stalactites reaching down from the ceiling and stalagmites growing up from the floor.

The same unenthusiastic guide told us that if we let a drop of water that was dripping from one of the stalactites fall on our heads, we would be blessed with good fortune. I could use every ounce of good fortune I could get so I nervously waited for a droplet to fall. Everyone cheered as it landed on my amber head.

Like a human train, we followed the guide within this underground maze. The deeper we went, the more open the cave became. Eventually we came to a room so large that an entire football stadium could fit inside of it. We were told to line up against the far wall.

"Is anyone afraid of the dark?" the monotone tour guide asked.

Most everyone said no. I looked over at the boy to see his expression. He looked as if he was brave enough.

After a click, the guide shut off the lights, and, let's just say, it was so pitch-black that it could cause us to become blind or so the guide said. Oh no! I hoped she was wrong as she continued to ramble. In the darkness, I found her even-toned voice to be the perfect match for this blinding cave tour.

Just when I thought blindness was setting in, she turned on a light in the distance which was shining upon beautiful, towering formations that looked like hardened drip sandcastles. I had never seen anything so unusual and fantastical. She turned on some other fixtures that illuminated what looked like a huge hanging cylindrical cage with spikes reaching down from the ceiling and mirroring spikes stretching to meet them like jaws on a shark.

The guide suggested that we sing together because the acoustics were supposedly superb. I didn't know what acoustics meant until everyone started to sing. I guessed that it meant sound traveling through space in a certain fashion, that fashion being magnificent. Everyone joined together and sang the same song I had heard at my nana's funeral. It seemed that everyone … in every place … knew this song.

Amazing grace how sweet the sound,
That saved a wretch like me.
I once was lost,
But now am found.
'Twas blind but now I see …

The words played in my head. It was true, just minutes ago, with no lights on, we were blind, but now with the lights on, we could see! The sound of people's voices echoed off the walls in a way that made them sound like a multitude of angels singing.

When the song was over, everyone clapped their hands and shared smiles. This cave tour was turning out to be much more amazing than I had anticipated.

By the looks of the outdoor building and the kooky old caveman, I had thought that Tuckaleechee Caverns wouldn't be just ho-hum, but I was wrong. This was not ho-hum at all, this was super-duper spectacular!

After some time, we traveled to the other

end of the cavern and found a waterfall that dribbled into a wishing well. Alice gave each of us a coin to make a wish. I wanted to make a worthy request so I wished that we would have a great trip, get home safely, and that Momma and Papa would hug and kiss each other again and have a good time being alone.

I know that was more than one wish, and that was against the rules, but still, maybe they would go hand in hand.

Abel and I skipped to the stairs and climbed up the steps that had once been so scary but now seemed silly. We made our way all the way to the gift shop where everything appeared necessary for me to purchase.

I didn't have any money though … so, there was that. I looked longingly at all the stuff that Momma would have called junk and wished that I had won the lottery so that I could spend away … with no care in the world.

"Grace! C'mon, let's go," Hope called.

I looked up and saw that everyone except Abel and I were exiting the once boring but now wondrous building. As we hopped up into the RV, Aunt Esther surprised us with fudge! It tasted like chocolate mixed with chocolate—my two favorite flavors.

My thumb and pointer finger sunk into the chunk as I slowly nibbled on the treat. I didn't want it to be gone quickly so I savored each bite.

"Where to now?" Hope asked.

"Through the woods and over the river to places you've never been …" Aunt Esther sang as Hope rolled her swirly eyes.

"Why won't you tell us?" Hope plead.

"Because," was all Aunt Esther would say, and it drove Hope nuts. Just like all the sloppy fudge on Abel's face was driving Alice nuts.

AND THE RV TRIP

✂ *Five* ✂

Fudge Faces

I must have looked like Abel with fudge all over my face too because Alice came by with a wet towel and wiped my fingers and face raw. Even though it was a bit rough, it felt good to be cleaned. Abel resisted more than I, but that didn't stop Alice from getting the job done.

I had no idea where we were headed, but even from within Ol' Tex, I could sense that the air smelled sweet. We came to a town called

Gatlinburg that was bustling with touristy activity. Gift shops lined the streets while a ski lift took passengers up alongside a mountain. An unmistakable urge to get out and walk through the streets came over me. I could see a bunch of arcades and candy stores that needed my coins … I mean, inspection.

After Aunt Esther found a big parking spot behind the first row of shoppes to keep Ol' Tex safe, we walked around. First thing we did was take that gondola ride up the side of the mountain. I rode with Aunt Esther, while Alice rode with Hope and Abel.

"Soooo? What do you think so far?" she asked.

"I think this is the coolest trip I've ever been on." I couldn't think of any other trips where we had had so much fun. Most of our trips as a family were picnics at waterfalls or sliding down rocks bouncing on our butts, but those were mostly day trips, not overnight stays like this vacation.

"Really? Well, that makes me glad," Aunt Esther grinned.

"Well, I'm glad, too," I said as a huge smile

spread across my cheeks.

The ride took us all the way to the tippy top of the mountain, then we swirled around and headed down. Going in this direction was a whole other feeling. I felt less safe barreling down the mountain, but I pretended to be brave.

Being brave or pretending to be brave can work up quite the appetite. After the ride was over, we found a cute little diner called "Perky's Place" and had some salty, curly french fries and greasy cheeseburgers. Boy, were they tasty. A tempting waffle-cone scent leaked out from the ice-cream shop next door.

"Smells like sundaes," Alice said.

"Sure does," Aunt Esther agreed.

We walked over to the "Sweet Swirl" and topped off our late lunch with delicious hot fudge, cherry topped ice-cream sundaes. Wasn't this the greatest? Caves, fudge, gondola rides, burgers, fries, and ice-cream sundaes??!! I know, right?

Happiness was bubbling over especially from inside my happy gurgling belly, and I was so glad that Aunt Esther and Alice had invited us on this trip. I wondered if Momma and Papa were having as much fun. They probably weren't because they weren't with us. And this was fun.

But, of course, it wasn't *all* fun …

Ol' Tex decided to not start when we got back to the lot where he was parked. Not that this was the worst place to be stuck, but, still, it was not fun seeing the look on Aunt Esther's and Alice's faces—they were worried.

As the sun was setting, Abel and I entertained ourselves by playing hopscotch. Hope made sure we didn't cheat while Alice fiddled around under the hood of Ol' Tex.

"Jumping Jehoshaphat!" Alice yelled as she jumped away at sparks that had shocked her.

"What happened?" I asked.

But Alice just shook her hand trying to make it not hurt. We gathered around Alice as she eventually gained her composure.

"What's the matter?" Hope asked.

"Oh, I don't know … this doohickey just shocked me is all."

Two big stocky men walked up and asked if they could be of assistance. Alice said she could handle it but these good, kind-hearted men simply *had* to help us.

"My name's Teddy Lee and this here is Mr. Tatz," the man introduced himself and his friend. Aunt Esther performed the polite formalities, introducing us.

"Maybe we'll just have a little look, ma'am? We'd hate to see y'all stranded all night," Mr. Tatz said.

Well, they gave it their best shot. They poked and prodded, fiddled and faddled, bumped their heads, and bruised their knuckles, trying to connect wires from here to there before they gave up.

"Well, I'll be dipped in turtle … poop," Teddy Lee exclaimed, utterly shocked that he wasn't able to fix Ol' Tex.

All the while, Abel was watching the two men, attempting to solve the problem on his own. He must have noticed a connection that looked like it wasn't together. Right before Teddy Lee and Mr. Tatz were about to leave, Abel asked, "What if we try this thingy?" and plugged a rectangular toggle into a corresponding shape.

Alice, out of curiosity, told Aunt Esther to try to start the engine. And wouldn't you know,

Ol' Tex turned right over. Everyone hooted and hollered for Abel, the mechanic.

"Well, I'll be darned!" Mr. Tatz said.

"How did you know to do that?" Hope asked.

"It just looked like two Legos that needed to be joined," Abel shrugged, as if it should have been common sense.

Hope looked astonished … shocked … yet proud.

"You're smart kid, real smart," Mr. Tucker said as he ruffled Abel's dark wavy hair.

"Good thinking, Abel," Alice congratulated him as we hopped aboard the now running RV.

"Looks like you're in good hands with that kid," the men tipped their caps to us before waving goodbye.

❦ • ❦

Time slid into slow mode as we traveled to who knows where. I could tell Hope wanted to ask where we were going, but she stopped herself, knowing the answer would not satisfy her curiosity. I was just happy to go along for the ride. I didn't care where we were headed, as long as we were going together … which made me miss Momma and Papa. We weren't together with them. I pictured how they looked when they were waving to us as we left. I had a sudden pang in my heart that hurt. I missed them.

I overheard Alice and Aunt Esther talking about how fortunate they were to have Abel here to get Ol' Tex running again. And how he might be some kind of genius. I looked over at Abel who was playing with his action-figures. He didn't look like a genius to me, but what did geniuses look like? I had always pictured them to be old scientists who blew stuff up, wore white lab coats, and had wild crazy silver hair.

Hope looked more genius-y with her round reading glasses and her hair up in a messy bun while studying one of her science books. But when it came down to it, it didn't matter what you looked like. I guess, it mattered what you could do with what you knew.

I heard *ba-bumps* and *ba-bumps* and *ba-bumps* under the tires of Ol' Tex.

"Do you hear those sounds?" Aunt Esther asked.

We all looked outside and saw that we were traveling over a clunky bridge.

"You know what that means?"

Abel squealed, "We are going over the river!"

"Look on the other side of the bridge!" Alice exclaimed.

We all sang together, "And through the woods!"

AND THE RV TRIP

ᥱᥱ *Six* ᥱᥱ

The Moon Maiden

The motion of the RV driving through the dark forest put me to sleep. I slipped into a serene state of being where I traveled to the moon on a super space highway. The man who supposedly lived on the moon was actually a quiet older lady sitting upon a rocking chair who used moonlight fibers to knit illuminated stars. After she finished knitting each star, she left a string on the end so she could send the star into space with a long hooked pole.

Instead of using the pole to catch fish, she used it to cast stars into the night sky. When they reached their home, they twinkled, letting her know that they were all settled. The more she knitted and threw into the cosmos, the more stars twinkled.

"Hello sunshine," she said to me in a wobbly yet soothing voice.

"Hello, ma'am."

"I'm the moon maiden."

"Hi!" I smiled because she was so pleasant to gaze upon. "I'm Grace Newton."

The moon maiden was a glowing silvery white silhouette the same hue as the moon. Her soft features reminded me of my nana. A pearly string draped around her neck and attached to her rounded glasses so she could see her work clearly, I presumed. She wore a long ruffled shadowed dress with lots of layers, topped with a sparkly apron. Her hair was tucked inside a dainty bonnet that framed her shadowed face.

I asked her if I could knit a star and she said, "Why yes, child, but you must be very attentive to each little shape. The stars are very special to me, each of them is unique … no two are alike."

"Yes ma'am," I said, hoping to knit a special, unique star properly.

She handed me two long needles and the illuminated yarn. "First you must close your eyes and imagine the shape in your mind."

I closed my eyes and pictured a happy, little smiling star.

"Now open your eyes and recreate the vision that you've imagined. Don't worry, it will come back to you as you knit."

She demonstrated her knitting for me as I followed her every move. Nana had done the same thing for me when she taught me how to sew. I worked for some time then before I knew it, I held the shape of a glowing star in my lap. My face shined in the star's light. I smiled as the star smiled back. The moon maiden was right, I created a star that *I* had imagined!

"Now it's time to name your star."

"I get to name him?"

"Of course, child! Every star has a name, just like you, and since you made the star, now you get to name it."

I looked at my smiling star and said, "I think I'll call him Happy."

"That's wonderful! Happy, are you ready to go home?"

The star smiled and bounced up and down. That must have meant, *yes*.

I didn't want to throw Happy into the infinite cosmos, yet. I wanted to stare at him longer but the moon maiden said it was time. *It was time … it was time to wake up …* I heard Hope saying to me as she shook my shoulder.

I didn't want to wake up. I wanted to play with my smiling star. I turned away and tried to picture the cute little star before my dream vanished like a vapor.

"We're here!" Hope said.

My eyes popped open. "Where?" I asked.

"Over the river and through the woods!" she said.

I looked outside the window. We were definitely in the woods. Tall trees surrounded us like a series of protective soaring soldiers as Abel zoomed by with his cape following his lead. Why was I always the last to wake? I hopped down from my perch to investigate where we had landed.

I stepped outside and into a campground in the middle of a green tall-tree forest. Smoke from a campfire in the distance greeted my senses. There was a fire pit waiting to be lit with a picnic table and a laundry line that separated us from the next-door neighbors. Alice and Aunt Esther were setting up the campsite with various hammocks, chairs, and strings of lights. Ol' Tex had a black and white striped awning that was rolled out over the side door. Green outdoor carpet was placed near the door to keep the dirt out, and a welcome mat was placed on top to create a second dirt barrier. Strings of white lights crisscrossed overhead so that when nighttime came, we could see.

This was sure to be a whole lot of fun! I thought …

… Until we heard a woman yelling next door. ***NELSON*** *stop doing this and* ***NELSON*** *stop doing that.* The way she said his name, ***NELSON***, over and over made the name sound terrible.

"C'mon, let's go check out the lake," Hope said diverting our attention away from

NELSON. Abel scurried on ahead of us as we walked along the graveled path. Some of the tall trees had leaves that flickered like golden coins in the breeze.

I picked up a couple of interesting, colored pebbles that looked good for skipping. I put them in my pocket for when we got to the lake. While walking obliviously, looking at this and that, I was somewhat stunned when we came to a suspension bridge that looked like it had been built by Tarzan.

"Wow!" we all marveled at the beauty that stood before us. As we walked over the wobbly, yet strong walking-bridge, I couldn't help but look up and down. The land had dropped into a deep valley with beautiful waterfalls in every direction. Stone walls covered in dangling ferns, vines, and flowers decorated this lush forest. Colorful butterflies and birds fluttered by as I carefully walked.

I couldn't believe we found such a sacred place to "camp". I felt like we had just found a new enchanted universe. Underneath us was a rapidly moving, rocky-bottomed blue river that dared us to fall. *No thanks*, I thought to myself, I'll just stay up here on this rickety bridge where it's nice and safe.

"Stop shaking the bridge!" Hope, holding on for dear life, scolded Abel who was jumping fearlessly across the planks.

Safely across the bridge, we looked back at the dramatic lush landscape. After taking a moment to remember this magical sight, we turned and ducked under drapes of lush greenery along the well-worn path.

From paradise, we approached the opposite … a cold, dark, bat-infested tunnel. To the right side of the entry was a sign that had a picture of a bunch of bats. I was *not* going any further. Bats and I didn't get along … not that I knew any bats personally, I just knew that they were bloodsuckers and that I needed all my blood in order to stay alive.

"C'mon, Grace," Hope prodded as I shook my head, already answering her.

Nope! I was not, I repeat, *NOT*, going to walk through that deep, dark, spooky tunnel. I knew what could happen in there. To say that I was a bit concerned was a gross understatement. Those bats would fly down, find my neck to suck my blood to death, like Dracula.

From the shadows, I spied a family of four walking through the tunnel with no care in the world. Were they aware of the obvious danger? I guess they weren't concerned because they seemed to have survived the tunnel of death, I mean the deathly tunnel of murderous bats, with all their blood. How could this be?

"C'mon, Grace, let's go," Hope called from within the tunnel's darkness. "Don't you want to get to the lake?"

"But, I'm scared," I said.

"Of what? Sleeping bats?"

"What if they wake up thirsty for blood? I need my blood or I'll die!" I told Hope.

She walked back out to coax me in. "These aren't vampire bats; they are just Tri-colored Bats, formerly known as the Eastern pipistrelle," Hope said as she regarded the plaque.

"How do you know?"

"I read the sign."

"Oh," I uttered, remembering said sign but all I had noticed were the pictures of the bats.

"We don't have all day to talk about these bats," Hope prodded while Abel bravely ran through the black tunnel without even a second of hesitation.

"C'mon, Grace," I heard Abel's voice call from the other side. If he made it through and all those other people made it through okay, I guess I should give it a shot.

Eventually my trembling feet started to move. It was frigid inside the tunnel, and I could hear the squeaking bats that were obviously not sleeping. For some reason, the tunnel smelled like frog poo. I had never smelled frog poo but if I did, I knew that this is how it would smell.

I looked up but couldn't see anything beyond the darkness. A drop of goo hit me in the forehead. I panicked and ran for the other side quicker than a comet racing through the starlit sky. What was that? I rubbed my forehead and scooped away a piece of clear jelly. It looked like a huge clear booger. My stomach turned. I felt like I was going to throw up.

Hope must have noticed my ailment. "What's the matter with you, Grace? You're fine."

"I think I'm going to throw up."

"Seriously? C'mon, look over there. Don't

you want to go see that?" Hope had me look into the distance, beyond the tunnel.

Nestled under a beautiful set of blue mountains, a clear bluish-green lake sparkled like a brilliant gem. Smooth blond rocks lined the perimeter of the giant pool-like lake. The sun shone down through the open sky making my sickly thoughts vanish. Kids splashed one another while parents spread out their picnics on blankets. Inflatable rafts floated around the center of the lake next to metal canoes holding the shadows of people off in the distance. I suddenly felt a whole lot better.

We walked around the lake looking for a less crowded place to park. I took off my shoes feeling the soft green grass before I dipped my toes into the refreshing water. The sand at the bottom of the lake was a light color making the water crystal clear. I desperately wanted to get all the way in, but my bathing suit was back in the RV. Not having the proper attire didn't stop Abel, who tore off his shirt and cape as he ran for the water then swam in his shorts.

Lucky ...

"I want to swim, too," I said to Hope as she

was staring at a boy who was walking into the water.

Flippantly, Hope said, "Go ahead."

What was wrong with Hope? Her eyes looked weird as she watched him. Any other day, she would have told me that I couldn't swim in my clothes, that I would have to go back and change into my swimsuit.

I decided to take advantage of her distractedness and went for a dip in my shorts and tank top. Abel and I splashed each other and jumped up and down, looking like lunatics, making waves. We were having a little too much fun when Hope finally came to her senses—I heard her call my name in her not so pleased voice.

"Grace, what are you doing? You're getting your clothes all wet!"

"But you said …" I started but stopped when she cut me off.

"You are going to make more laundry for us to do."

I wasn't sure she was right about that. The clothes I was wearing were already dirty and were likely getting cleaner in the lake, I surmised. She signaled for me to get out of the water. Obediently, I walked up to her but her gaze shifted behind me, when I heard a boy say, "Hi".

I turned around to see the same boy Hope had been staring at before smiling at her.

I turned back to Hope who had a sheepish grin on her face and suddenly I became invisible again. Thankful for the diversion, I ran back into the lake and splished and splashed with Abel.

ೋ *Seven* ೋ

Hope's Dream Boy

Hope stood still, unsure if she should say more. The boy was tall and tan with longish dark hair. It had blond streaks from the sun that made his blue eyes sparkle like blooming nebulae. He must be older than she, Hope thought. He stood tall with the onset of muscles beginning to take shape under his flawless skin. Even though it was obvious that he was interested, he appeared slightly aloof as he casually skipped a few rocks into the lake.

"What's your name?" he asked as he walked closer.

"Hope Newton," she answered.

Hope wasn't used to getting attention from any boys back home. They all knew that she was a studious bookworm on track for an out-of-this-world career.

This guy knew nothing about her, other than her name.

"Hi, Hope Newton, I'm Stefan."

To Hope, the name Stefan was now the most sensational name she had ever heard. For one, she had never heard such an exotic name from such an attractive boy. All the boys back home were named Junior, Tater, Buddy, Jimmy Bob, or Dudley. And two, he, *Stefan*, was talking to her as if she was pretty. Hope knew she was pretty to her mother, family, and friends, but to have another random person act as if he thought so too was extra special.

"Are you here with your family?"

Hope nodded.

"Me, too. Well, actually just my dad and my annoying younger brother. My parents are divorced so my dad takes us for a couple of weeks here and there, and we usually go camping or something like that."

"Oh," Hope said not knowing how to respond.

"That your sister and brother?"

Hope nodded. "Yes … they're younger."

"No way," he said in a teasing manner.

Hope sneaked a smile.

"There it is. I was hoping I could get you to smile."

Hope smiled even bigger.

"It's very pretty; you should smile all the time."

"How do you know I don't?"

"Because I've been watching you for a couple minutes and this was the first time you did it."

"You were watching me?"

"Yeah … Believe it or not most of the people here are either really young or really old … not that many people around our age. It's hard being the only sixteen-year-old on vacation. You know what I mean." He said this as if Hope too was sixteen.

Hope was thirteen, but to most people she looked every bit of sixteen or even seventeen. "Oh well, I'm not sixteen, I'm …" she began to say but then thought that if she told him her real age, he might not want to talk to her anymore.

"Fifteen?" he guessed.

Hope shrugged and went along with his assumption thinking that she'd probably never see him again anyway.

Abel ran up shivering. "I'm cold Hope; do you have a towel?"

"No, I didn't think you guys were going to go swimming. Let's go back to Ol' Tex and get one from Aunt Esther or Alice."

Hope gave Stefan a look that said, *sorry … gotta go.*

"I'll walk you guys back if you want. I got nothing else to do."

Abel looked suspicious but Hope said, "Oh, okay."

"What about Grace?" Abel asked.

"C'mon Grace, let's go!" Hope called.

AND THE RV TRIP

❦ *Eight* ❦

Dog Farts

Abel and I shivered as we galloped back to our campsite. We walked up to find Aunt Esther and Alice talking with a man and his dog. The man was obviously old, but the wretched, terribly ugly dog looked to be about a thousand. Abel and I stood shivering by the warm fire that was already going strong.

The dog was scratching itself and biting its skin then yelping loudly in pain at its self-inflicted wounds. With angry brown eyes, the dog looked up at us kids, growled then went back to chewing his scabby skin and crying out in pain. With no fur, except for the tuft of blackish white poofy spikes on top of his head, the pet looked more like a cursed creature. As I came to such a conclusion, I realized that this was the ugliest dog I had ever seen.

The old man who must have been the dog's owner ignored the growls and cries as he continued to talk and listen to Alice and Aunt Esther. He explained, "If y'all should need anything, come find me and Beverly next door."

"Oh, is Beverly your wife?" Aunt Esther asked.

"No, she's my RV."

"Your RV is named Beverly?"

"Yup, we been together 'bout ten years."

"Well, I'll be darned. You named your camper, too … this here is Ol' Tex," Aunt Esther introduced our camper to the old man.

"Howdy do," the man said before he smiled down at me.

"Howdy do, sir," I replied for Ol' Tex.

"Y'all can call me Mr. Box," he said as he nodded.

I smiled up at him. Tucked beneath a few friendly wrinkles, his kind, milky brown eyes smiled.

"C'mon, Stinky, let's go on home," he called.

As he tugged on the leash, Stinky yelped then let out a long, stinky, extra smelly fart. *Ewwwww* … That dog *was* stinky.

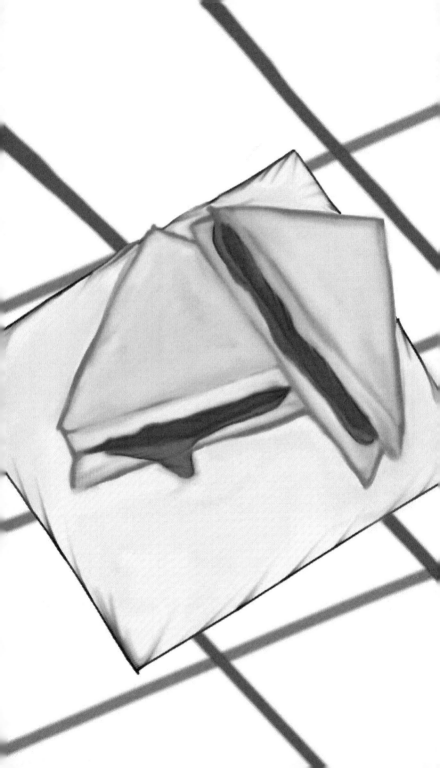

✿ *Nine* ✿

PBJ's

"You guys must have found the lake!" Alice announced.

"What makes you think that?" Aunt Esther chimed in.

"Oh, I don't know … maybe it's the soaked clothes and muddy feet? C'mon let's get you two cleaned up before we eat lunch." Abel and I followed Alice around to a pole with a spigot. She brought over the hose and cleaned off our feet then sprayed our bellies and faces as we giggled and splashed each other.

Lunch was peanut butter and jelly sandwiches, homemade apple chips, green grapes, leftover Danish Puff, and pink lemonade. I looked over at Hope who scolded Abel for having smudges of jelly around his mouth. She plopped down a napkin in front of him as she rolled her eyes.

"*NELSON*!!! Stop eating the dog food!" we heard coming from the other campsite. "You're going to get worms crawling out of your poop shoot, *NELSON*!"

We all began to laugh.

"See *NELSON*, if you keep this up, you'll be the laughing stock wherever you go," the mom said in her whiney voice.

I guess she heard us laughing. And then we heard a dog yelping … Stinky must be eating himself again, I thought.

A couple of other campers stopped by to say hello. They were a pale, middle-aged couple with snarky smiles. The man was super tall and the woman was super short, but I couldn't take my eyes away from the tiny dog that was strapped onto the man's upper body, like a baby. The pup looked so relaxed in its contraption. The strange sight made me laugh … it's not every day that you see a tiny dog in a baby harness strapped to an old man's chest.

"Howdy, y'all," the man greeted. "Welcome to Camp Igottapoopee."

"Now you stop it, silly, that's not the name," his wife scolded.

"Oh, sorry, that's just our little nickname we have for this slice of paradise we got here," he clarified. "Name's Marty, Margo, and Punky Morsel … actually, *my* name is Marty, she's Margo, the pup is named Punky, and our last name is Morsel."

"I'm sure they figured that out for themselves," Margo said while caressing the sleepy dog's down-turned paws.

"Well, it certainly is a pleasure to meet you. My name is Esther, this is Alice, and these are my nieces and nephew, Hope, Grace, and Abel."

"Fine lookin' youngins you got there. You'll be wanting to come to the movie tonight, won't ya?"

"Movie?" Abel and I blurted.

"Well, sure! Every Tuesday is outdoor movie night. Up at the pavilion, 'round 8:00 o'clock everyone shows up for s'mores, popcorn, and a movie. Tonight's show will be Chocolate Charlie something ... it's sure to be a 'reel' crowd pleaser." He used air quotes around his punny joke.

"Oh! I want to go!" I said.

"Me too! Me too!" Abel echoed.

"Can we? Can we?" I asked Aunt Esther and Alice.

"I don't see why not!"

"Yay!" we cheered.

Abel and I shared our excitement across the table from each other while Hope showed little expression, as usual. She quietly nibbled on her apple chips while daydreaming about something.

After we finished cleanup from lunch, I asked if we could go back to swim at the lake. But Aunt Esther and Alice had a better idea. They rented bicycles so we could ride around the campground and up into the trails that took us through what I am now choosing to call the giant's forest. The trees were so tall, I bet one of them was the beanstalk that Jack used to climb all the way up to the giant's house. Plus, as we rode, I swore I could hear *fee-fi-fo-fum* echoing off the tree trunks as we passed. As we circled the trails, we quickly descended.

I could hear water rushing as we rode down the trail that took us to the bottom of the waterfall valley. Along the rushing river, it was impossible to speak without yelling. But we had little to say because of the sights and sounds were all that we wanted to see and hear. As I took in at all the rich beauty in every emerald green grass blade, brown baby pinecone, multicolored wildflower, green mossed covered tree trunk, smooth skipping pebble, I found a new appreciation for nature. What could be better?

I'll tell you what isn't better … having to ride uphill all the way back to our campsite. What seemed like took us minutes to get to the bottom of the trail, took us hours to go back up. Needless to say, our legs hurt.

As we pedaled toward our campsite, I saw Stinky and Mr. Box sitting near his RV, Beverly.

She was a super, shiny, stainless steel beauty with a red and white striped awning.

The opposite of a super, shiny, beauty was Stinky who was gnawing on his back while Mr. Box was carving something out of a piece wood. I looked around his campsite and saw a bunch of other wooden carvings. I circled around to get a better look at them.

His milky eyes looked up at me for a second then went back to his work. I stood gawking at all the fine details on each piece while he sat quietly whittling away. Stinky made enough noise for the two of them.

I looked around for Hope and the rest of the gang, but they must have biked back to our neighboring site.

"Whatdya think?" he asked after Stinky briefly hushed.

"Huh? Oh, uh," I nervously stuttered.

"You can come look at them closer if you want," he gestured with his knife. Even though he was holding a sharp weapon, he didn't scare me. I walked over and looked at a lifelike eagle made from wood, a bear with some chubby cubs, a squirrel, a deer, and even a chicken that reminded me of Noodle. I missed my Noodle. I hoped Momma was taking good care of him. But he really didn't need that much, he *was* a chicken, after all.

"Like chickens?" Mr. Box asked.

"Yes, I have a pet chicken back home."

"You do now, do ya?" he said.

"Yup."

"What kind?"

"He's a yellow kind," I informed him.

"A yellow chicken, huh. Boy, girl?"

"Boy," I said as if I knew.

"Oh, a rooster! What's his name?"

"Noodle," I said.

He smiled and said, "Noodle, eh ... that's a good name for a chicken."

"Thanks."

Stinky yelped then rolled over to attack another area of his skin.

"A name says a lot, you know," he said thoughtfully.

I thought about when Aunt Esther told me how Hope, Abel, and I were named, understanding his meaning.

"Look over yonder to old Stinky girl ...

either I am some sort of seer or naming her Stinky made her stink. Who knows? But don't ya ever wonder how so many people seem to match their names?"

I looked over at Stinky, thinking that she was a boy until now. But yeah, she too was appropriately named—she stunk.

"What was your name again?" he asked.

"Um, Grace," I answered.

"Um Grace? That's a name I ain't never heard before."

"It's just Grace, actually."

"Oh, I see. I should have known. You look like a Grace."

"How?" I asked.

"Well, I'll tell ya … all the Grace's I ever met were nice as could be and smart as an elephant."

"An elephant? I didn't know that elephants were smart."

"Oh yes, very smart. Don't you know that an elephant never forgets? They got to be pretty smart to have brains big enough to hold everything they've ever learned. Wouldn't you agree?"

Wow, I thought about all the things I had forgotten. I wondered if I knew even half as much as I had not remembered. I couldn't even remember all the things that I had forgotten. I guess elephants were smart.

Hope pedaled up and said, "Oh, that's where you are."

"Hi, Hope," I said.

"Hope, huh? That's a great name, too. All the Hope's I've ever met were studious and notably responsible," Mr. Box said to Hope's surprise.

"What's studious?" I asked.

"I'm gunna tell you but once I do, you can never forget, ya hear?"

"Kay," I agreed.

"Someone who studies a lot."

"How'd you know?" I asked shocked at his accuracy.

"Told you, names are important."

Hope looked suspicious but also intrigued.

"We have to go help Aunt Esther and Alice make supper so we can go to the movie on time," Hope said to me as she watched Mr. Box carve.

I didn't want to leave, but I really didn't want to miss the movie either. He was a really nice man and all, but I had to be on time for that movie!

"Stinky, Beverly, and I will be here whenever y'all wanna visit," he said assuring us. He must have understood how important that movie was for us to see.

"Okay, bye, Mr. Box," I said.

"It's Benjamin Franklin Box … my full name, that is," he said.

"Oh, uh …" I didn't know what to say next.

"Don't worry … there'll always be next time."

AND THE RV TRIP

✿ *Ten* ✿

Movie Night

Under a string of warm, white lights, we dined at dusk. We had made a big pot of spaghetti and sauce for dinner along with a side of greens and toasted garlic bread. I slurped up my noodles like I hadn't eaten for weeks. I couldn't wait for s'mores, popcorn, and a movie. Hope and I did the dishes while Aunt Esther and Alice cleaned up and put away the food so that ornery bears wouldn't come in and steal our food.

We headed out on our bicycles to the pavilion. When we got there, it seemed that everyone else in the whole campground had showed up as well. Even the boy Hope had been staring at by the lake was there. He was definitely staring at Hope, too.

Abel and I cared about one thing—s'mores and how many we could make and eat in mass consumption. We foraged through the woods looking for the perfect marshmallow roasting sticks, fought over whose was better, then exchanged them to only end up with the original sticks that we had found.

I plunged my hand into the plastic bag of soft white marshmallows, pulled one out, and stabbed it with my stick. Flames reached up as I held it over the fire, letting it catch a little heat before I blew it out. If the marshmallow was burnt or scorched, it would be no good. If it wasn't in the fire long enough, it would be too cold on the inside and too raw-marshmellowy, meaning not great. I took my s'more making very seriously.

"Aw man!" Abel dropped his marshmallow into the fire.

"Get another one," I said as I carefully placed my cooked-to-perfection marshmallow between two graham crackers and a hunk of chocolate.

I bit down on the glorious dessert and chewed the delightful flavors. What a great taste! After I finished a whole square, I grabbed another marshmallow to toast.

"Aw man!" Abel dropped another marshmallow into the fire.

"Get another one," I said again, laser focused on my next treat.

"Will you help me, Grace? I keep dropping mine."

I looked at his sad eyes, finished roasting my marshmallow, and gave it to him.

"Here you go, take mine. I'll roast another one."

"Thanks, Grace!" he said as he chomped down on his treat.

After one more, I couldn't take anymore s'mores. They were super delicious, but there's only so many s'mores one could eat. That limit did not exist for Abel. He kept eating them all night. If Momma were here, she would have made him stop. And if Hope were paying attention to someone other than that boy, she would have said something, too. *I* was too busy wanting to watch the movie that was about to start.

I found Aunt Esther and Alice who had arranged a lovely nighttime picnic, snacking on some popcorn as the movie began.

Where was Hope? I looked around and found her standing face to face with that boy … talking.

Hmmmmm … what were they talking about? I wondered.

❧ *Elevn* ❧

Goals

"I can't wait to get back to my mom's though," Stefan said.

"Why?" Hope asked.

"I'll be getting my driver's license. My dad's been giving me driving lessons, and I would have to say, I'm a pretty good driver."

"Is that so?" Hope said with a cynical expression.

"What? You don't believe me?"

"I don't believe most everything."

"Oh, you're one of those, huh," Stefan said while scrutinizing Hope's statement.

"What?" she asked.

"A skeptic."

"I'm not so sure about that …" Hope shrugged.

"Spoken like a true skeptic," Stefan smiled.

"I don't like to be assigned absolutes."

Stefan's brow raised. "Well, *I guess* I'll just have to prove it to you then, huh?"

"Prove what?"

"That you're a skeptic."

"How can you prove that?" Hope wondered.

"Do you believe that you are not a skeptic?"

Hope shrugged. "I'm not sure that's correct. I generally don't believe things until proven otherwise."

"Exactly," Stefan had a smug expression.

"What?" Hope asked.

"I proved that you are a skeptic."

"No, you just proved the likeliness of me being a skeptic."

Stefan shook his head. "What are you some sort of scientist or something?"

"That's the plan."

"For real? You think you could be some sort of rocket scientist or something?" he said as if she was surely joking.

"Actually, I do. I want to be an astronaut like Sally Ride."

Stefan laughed and said, "Oh, okay."

"You know *you* sound awfully doubtful. You must be a skeptic, as well."

"I doubt that! What kind of schooling do you need to be an astronaut anyway?" he asked thinking that she probably didn't know.

"Well, it depends on if you go the military route or civilian. I plan to go the civilian route because I think it will get me there faster. I would need a degree in engineering with a focus on mathematics. I could also study some specific science if I wanted to know more, but it takes more than brains to be an astronaut. In order to be even looked at, I must have 20/20 vision, blood pressure not more than 140/90 in a sitting position, and a height of between 62 and 75 inches. I'm already tall enough so I just have stay in good shape, physically and mentally." Hope said all this as if it was common knowledge.

Stefan looked impressed but still a little dubious. "Okay, *well* … uh … you make wanting to get a driver's license sound pretty lame."

Hope laughed. "Hey, I haven't even gotten *that* far, so you're one step ahead of me."

"Have you been working on your driving skills?" he asked. "When's your birthday?"

Suddenly Hope had nothing to say. She popped a graham cracker into her mouth and munched on it longer than necessary so as not to answer his question.

"Well?"

"It just passed," Hope said, thinking quickly.

"Oh, well then, happy belated birthday!"

"Thanks, I should go see if my Aunt needs me for anything."

"Want me to come?"

"Nah, but thanks," Hope said trying to discourage him from following her, not because she didn't like him, but because she *did* like him and she didn't want anyone to slip up by saying her real age.

It's not as if she lied, she reminded herself,

however, she didn't clear up his misunderstanding when she first met him, either.

⚙ *Twelve* ⚙

Bumble Bears

When the movie started, I became lost in the fantasy of exploring the inside of a wondrous chocolate factory. Abel and I laid on the blanket, mindlessly foot wrestling as we watched flashes of chocolate rivers, giant gobstoppers, and gassy floating bubbles. After it was over, I realized that I had fallen asleep … when Alice woke me. Abel had also fallen asleep by the looks of his eyes when I had tried to focus on them.

"It was a long day! We will have another long, fun day tomorrow, too." Alice promised as we groggily pedaled back to our campsite.

Abel and I settled into each of our opposite sides of the bed. The sleep that had taken over before was still heavy in my head.

So, there I was in the middle of a fantastic dream, when I heard a noise. It became part of my dream for an instant and then it was so loud I knew those sounds were not meant for my mid-night-trances.

I shot straight up in bed and peeked out of the window. I saw exactly what you don't want to see when you're half asleep.

A BEAR!!!!

"It's going to be okay, just stay quiet." Aunt Esther whispered. "As soon as he realizes that there is nothing here, he will leave," she assured us.

The bear came closer to Ol' Tex; he sniffed around the door, deciding if he should break in. Oh no! What if a big bear barged in here, roared until our ears popped, used his big bear claws to rip Ol' Tex apart, and then all of us? I wanted to cry. I looked over at Abel, expecting to see him trembling, but he stood bravely, quiet as Aunt Esther had told us to be. If Abel could be quiet, so could I. I heard the bear huff like he was frustrated then the voice of Mr. Box scolding the bear.

"Now you go on and git! Git on outta here!" he yelled. Out of the window, I saw Mr. Box holding a rifle by his side but not pointed at the bear. Stinky was by his side, looking confused about her role in this bear scare. He raised his arms and yelled again as the bear tumbled off the stairs.

"Go on, this ain't your house. Now you go on home, ya hear!" he yelled as Stinky half-barked and half-yelped.

I think the foul stench that Stinky put off made the bear go away more than the yelling from Mr. Box.

Boy, was I happy that Mr. Box and smelly Stinky were our neighbors.

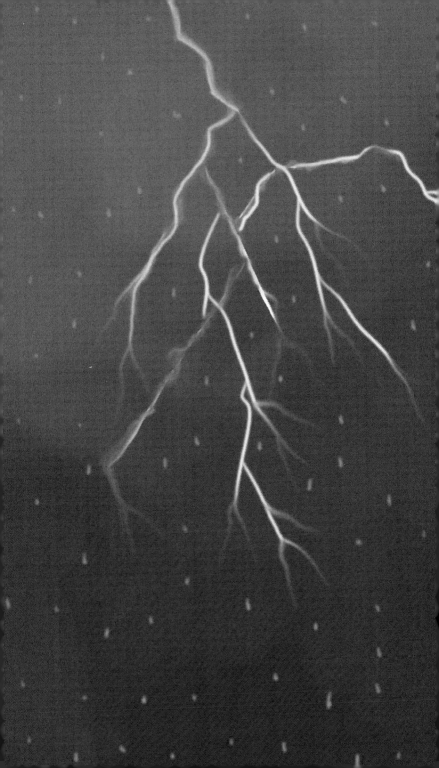

✑ *Thirteen* ✑
Burial Mounds

A rumbling thunder along with a pounding downpour of rain woke me in the morning but not before waking everyone else first, of course. Water was coming down in buckets while the sky blasted bolts of electricity through the air. I sat at the table wondering if we would be able to have fun today. Ol' Tex suddenly shrank into a tiny little overstuffed prison. What could we do all day inside?

Hope was busy with her big science books that she reread every couple of months. Abel only needed his action figures to play with for hours, where I was left with nothing—No Mazie, no Noodle, no sewing, no nothing. Lumps was a fine stuffed bunny, but after a while, I needed something more entertaining.

I dramatically threw myself on the couch and loudly sighed.

"What's the matter, Grace?" Aunt Esther asked.

"I'm bored."

"It's perfect spooky reading weather. How about you read a book?" She held up a thick hardcover book as a roll of thunder shook Ol' Tex.

I looked at her like she was crazy. I hated reading. Reading was always a struggle. I liked hearing the stories that were in books, but when it came time for me to read the actual words, that was an impossible thing. The letters that were supposed to make certain sounds looked different to me every time I looked at them.

"No thanks," I politely said.

"What about poems?" she asked. "Poems

are perfect if you hate to read."

I tried to think of a way to tell her how I felt, but all I could think to say was, "Nah".

She opened up the book and thumbed through some of the pages, looked back up at my bored face and asked, "Do you have trouble reading?"

I shrugged.

"You know, I struggled with reading too. In fact, I hated books until I found the right one."

"Which book was it?"

"This one right here! There are so many poems in it; I could read them over and over and still feel like I was reading them for the first time. In fact, through poetry, I actually learned to read. You see, a poem is a story that can paint a picture. Have you ever seen a picture?"

"Yes," I said.

"Have you ever seen a picture inside your mind?"

"I guess so."

"How?" she asked.

I shrugged.

"Well, would you like for me to paint a picture inside your mind?"

"Sure."

"Want me to read you a poem?"

Ugh … that wasn't what I had in mind. "If you want," I shrugged and said.

Aunt Esther flipped through the book and found one that made her eyebrows raise. "Oh, this one is perfect for today." She looked over to the window then lit some candles to set the mood. "This is a poem about Indian burial mounds written by Philip Freneau, ready?"

"Yes," I said. "But hold on, I need Lumps." I scurried up the bunk and grabbed my stuffed bunny then sat waiting for her to begin.

Her voice sounded eerie as she began to recite the poem.

In spite of all the learned have said,
I still my old opinion keep;
The posture, that we give the dead,
Points out the soul's eternal sleep.

"He's saying, whatever you've heard about the dead, think again," Alice explained.

Apparently Alice knew this poem well.

AND THE RV TRIP

Not so the ancients of these lands—
The Indian, when from life released,
Again is seated with his friends,
And shares again the joyous feast.

His imaged birds, and painted bowl,
And venison, for a journey dressed,
Bespeak the nature of the soul,
Activity, that knows no rest.

"When the Native Indians die, they are not really dead."

"Really? What are they then, zombies?" Abel asked. Apparently Abel was listening, too.

"Not exactly, here, let's see," Aunt Esther continued.

His bow, for action ready bent,
And arrows, with a head of stone,
Can only mean that life is spent,
And not the old ideas gone.

"Can you picture the Indian's bow and arrow bent, ready to shoot with arrow heads made from stone?" Alice asked.

"Yes, I can now," I said.

> *Thou, stranger, that shalt come this way,*
> *No fraud upon the dead commit—*
> *Observe the swelling turf, and say*
> *They do not lie, but here they sit.*

Alice said, "If you ever find an Indian burial mound, don't touch it or harm it because the spirit is there sitting—not lying around as if dead."

A bolt of lightning and a blast of thunder shook the ground under Ol' Tex and made me scream. I jumped up from the table accidentally knocking over one of the candles.

"Uh-oh!" I said as Alice quickly grabbed the stick before the flame could do any damage.

"It's okay, I got it," she said.

As she was cleaning up, I remembered the last thought I had before the lightning struck. I had pictured an Indian burial mound, deep within the woods, with spirits hovering around it. Aunt Esther was right; these words did paint a picture. I guess my face was also quite a sight because Aunt Ester said, "How about we do something a little less frightening?"

"I … I … I'm not scared," I said, but wasn't sure if that was true.

"We'll finish the rest of the poem on a not so spooky day, okay?" Alice said. "How about a game of checkers? Do you want to play?"

"Will you let me win?" I asked.

"Of course! If you actually beat me, I will *let* you win."

"Poop."

"C'mon, let's play anyway."

"Okay …" I got out the game and set up the pieces. Before I knew it, half of the day was gone, and it wasn't even raining outside anymore. Hope and Abel were outside seeing if the bear had done any real damage to our site. I never won a game, but I had fun trying.

"Let's go to the lake!" Abel said.

∽ *Fourteen* ∾
Mermaids

With naughty clouds scrambling out of the sky and the commanding sun beaming, warming the air, the lake seemed like the best place to be right about now. Even Aunt Esther and Alice put on their suits, packed a picnic, and went with us to the lake.

Walking over the suspension bridge, surrounded by walls of waterfalls could never get old. If I were to see this sight every day for the rest of my life, I would forever be in awe of its magnificence. Tall trees draped with additional flowering foliage held sparkling drops of the waterfalls essence, giving each trumpet, petal, leaf, and cone a shimmering quality. This place needed nothing additional to make it appear magical … It just was.

When we got to the bat tunnel, I tried to stay brave. I mean, I *had* just walked over a rickety-rockity bridge with no fear, so it's not like I'm a total sissy. But as I was halfway through the deep, dark bat tunnel, I ran to the other end faster than Abel had ever run, or so it felt, and came out of the other side with my courage lost inside my beating chest.

At least I didn't throw up.

When we got to the sand, I chucked off my shoes, threw off my shirt and shorts, then ran into the water like I was on fire. The cool water soothed my overactive fear. I opened my eyes under the surface, seeing everything through a blurry filter. Sparkling emerald grasses on the bottom of the lake swayed back and forth mixed with the light blue topaz water. It looked mythical—like where mermaids lived.

I imagined the beautiful creatures with their wavy sparkling hair and long turquoise fins swimming through underground caves. I put my legs together and pumped them like I was a real mermaid, holding my breath for what felt like an eternity. I came up gasping for air, realizing that I was almost in the middle of the lake and I couldn't touch the bottom. Suddenly the shore felt like a million miles away, and my body weighed two thousand tons.

I went back under and sank toward the bottom of the lake, wondering if I had the strength to swim all the way back when I saw Mazie swimming gracefully toward me. Mazie wasn't inside the puddle this time; she was a mermaid who was talking to me through her bubbles.

"You can do this! Don't be afraid."

"But I'm scared. What if I drown?"

"I will never let you drown! See, I'm right here with you, and I can help you swim extra fast. Just like before when you thought you were a mermaid."

"But, I was just pretending," I explained.

"Keep pretending then. C'mon we'll swim together," she urged.

I watched Mazie flutter her tail as I wiggled my legs, popping up to the surface. I grabbed a gulp of fresh air, then swam alongside Mazie, the mermaid. When I made it to where I could stand, I looked back for Mazie who had swum away already. She was extra fast. *Thank you Mazie*, I thought to myself.

AND THE RV TRIP

⚬✺ *Fifteen* ✺⚬

Swimming Through Space

"I had a dream about you last night," Stefan said to Hope as they stood near the lakeside concession stand.

"About me? What about me?" Hope couldn't help but blush as she was spreading sunblock on her face and shoulders.

"I dreamed that we were driving in my car going to who knows where. I think we were near a meadow or something like that. But anyway, I dreamed that we were driving … actually, only I was driving … and we were listening to some music, and there was this song playing about this guy named, Major Tom."

"Huh? Who's that?"

"Not sure, but suddenly we stopped because we had hit something … probably a rock. But instead of getting out to check, the car literally turned into a rocket and we shot up into the sky like a space shuttle … but we were still in the car."

Hope was intrigued. Even she hadn't ever had a dream about herself being in outer space. All of her imaginary interstellar trips took place while she was awake. "Then what happened?"

"The car broke away in parts floating away from us. We had no suits on and could only breathe by kissing each other."

Hope blushed. She had never been kissed and didn't know how or if she was ready for such a big step. What would happen if he kissed her?

◌᷅Sixteen ᷄◌

Aiming Practice

From the safety of the shore, I stood looking out across the lake. Abel snuck up behind me and squirted my head with his water gun. I quickly ran after him, grabbed it, then squirted him back. He used his hands to splash me as I barely wetted him with the nearly useless weapon.

"I'm done with this," I said as I ran off.

We decided to take turns aiming at soda cans, trying to knock them off a wall near the concession stand. Abel had good aim like I did. But someone else had even better aim. I watched the boy that Hope had been eyeing peck her on the cheek. I dropped the gun.

"Hey, give it to me if you don't want it," Abel whined.

"Abel look! That boy just kissed Hope."

Without even a second to ponder, Abel grabbed the gun from the ground, ran over, and started squirting the boy in the head.

"Hey!" he called while trying to block the assault with his hands.

"Abel stop!" Hope yelled.

"He kissed you," Abel said as if this was a good reason to punish such a crime.

Hope blushed. She looked over at Aunt Esther and Alice who had turned around to check on all the ruckus. The boy looked at Hope, wiped off drops of water that had landed on his puckered lips, smiled, and said something quietly before turning to leave.

"And stay away!" Abel called as the boy left.

"Abel! Don't talk that way to him!" Hope yelled as she ran away with her cheeks glowing like fireballs.

"What's her problem?" Abel asked me.

"She's boy crazy, I think."

"Boy crazy? What's that?"

"I think it's when you like boys more than anything else."

"Hope?"

"Yup."

"Boys?"

"Uh-huh."

"Huh …" he said while looking like he was trying to understand this ailment of Hope's and how to cure her of it.

After about fifteen seconds, we went back to our shooting game, forgetting all about Hope's disease.

AMAZING GRACE NEWTON

❧ *Seventeen* ❧
Hope's Despair

Hope was already back at the campsite when the rest of us returned. She looked strange. She was holding a book, but she wasn't reading the pages. I had never before seen this look on her face. It was like she wanted to get away from here but couldn't leave. Maybe she wanted to stay *here*, just not with us.

"What's the matter, Hope?" I asked.

She turned away and refused to answer me.

"Are you mad at me?"

"Just leave me alone."

I looked around and thought that this was not exactly the best place to be if you wanted to be alone.

"What did I do?" I asked knowing that Abel was the one who had squirted her boyfriend with the gun.

She slammed the book down and said, "Nothing!" as she stormed out of the door.

"Well," I said, not sure of what to think or say next.

"Don't worry, Grace. One day you'll understand," Aunt Esther said as she was climbing down from her overhead bunk.

"When?"

"When you're boy crazy, too."

"Me, boy crazy? Never ... yuck."

The thought of a boy kissing me gave me the heebie-jeebies. I felt like I was back in that bat tunnel. *Gross.*

"I never want to kiss a boy," I stated.

"Ha! Say it again, I have got to get this recorded," Aunt Esther said as she laughed.

"I never want to kiss a boy! I never want to

kiss a boy!" I repeated.

"What's wrong with kissing a boy?" Abel asked. "I'm a boy and Nana and Momma and Papa kisses me," Abel misspoke.

"You're not a boy … you're my brother … that's different."

"Am too a boy," Abel insisted.

"Nuh-uh!" I said.

"Yes-huh!"

Aunt Esther jumped in and said, "Guess what?"

"What?" Abel and I asked.

"You're both right! And you both need to get washed up for supper."

Alice herded us to the hose and sprayed us clean. We shivered in our towels waiting to dry before getting dressed.

We gathered around the picnic table that had two strings of lights crisscrossing overhead. Under an open sky while crickets chirped in the bushes, we sat and passed around big bowls of yummy homemade fixins. What a great way to dine, I thought.

As we were eating supper we heard a screech, a thump, a loud yelp, then some yelling. I shot up from the picnic table and ran toward the commotion. I didn't get too far because right away, I saw Stinky, for the first time ever, looking peaceful ... bleeding to death.

The boy Hope had been kissing was standing next to a man, most likely his father, who was yelling, saying that people need to take better care of their dogs, that they shouldn't just let them wander around in the streets. But what he was really saying was that he felt guilty for running over Stinky.

Mr. Box's face looked so sad. No words spilled from his trembling mouth; however, heartbroken tears dripped from his weeping eyes.

All of the other man's words were drowned by the shock and sadness welling up from inside Mr. Box. I knew this feeling of sorrow. I slowly walked over to him and put my hand inside his rough grip. I looked up into his milky eyes and watched as they registered the horrible accident. His hand gently squeezed mine.

Hope stood over Stinky in shock while the boy kept saying how sorry he was.

"I'm so sorry sir, I didn't see your dog." He did look genuinely remorseful.

Hope said nothing, standing over Stinky.

Mr. Box started to waver in his stance. The boy and his father grabbed him before he could fall. After steadying him, they walked Mr. Box over to a chair.

The boy's father changed his tone, sensing Mr. Box's grief. He pulled out his wallet and grabbed a stack of bills and offered Mr. Box a sum of money to pay for the damages. Mr. Box shook his head. The man insisted that he take the money, but Mr. Box wouldn't so the man handed it to me and said, "Please, when he is able to accept my deepest apologies, give this to him on behalf of Stefan and me."

I held the money and told Mr. Box that I would not leave him. Abel came and sat next to us with his arm around Mr. Box's leg. For once, instead of his cape flying in the wind, it was solemnly draped around his back. Sometimes being super meant being calm and quiet.

Aunt Esther and Alice grabbed a couple of towels and white sheets to wrap Stinky up, all except for her face. For the first time, I saw what she must have looked like as a sweet little black puppy—so sweet and calm. She looked like a shrouded puppy dog angel.

Poor Stinky, poor Mr. Box … I wiped some tears away with our holding hands. I looked up at his watery eyes as he looked down at mine.

"It's okay … it's okay," was all he could say. *Poor Mr. Box* was all I could think.

ഏ*Eighteen* ഏ
Older Problems

Stefan felt horrible. The guilt that wrapped around him smothered his soul. "Hope, you have to know that that was an accident. I would never kill any dog on purpose."

Hope was quiet which was even harder for Stefan. He was trying to reassure her about his true character, but truthfully, what he was looking for, was someone to make him feel better about the mishap. Deep down, he knew that he had been careless as he drove. All he wanted to do was impress Hope as he drove by her campsite in his dad's fancy, cool car, but all he achieved was looking like a major doo doo head.

Hope moved away from Stefan as he nudged closer.

"Please Hope, please don't do this to me. I feel terrible, I don't know what to do!"

Hope exhaled. "I know you didn't mean to kill Stinky, but I'm just not ready to talk to you right now," Hope said through a brain fog, consisting of not knowing how to feel or what to say. She liked Stefan … a lot, but in this moment, when the dog was accidentally killed by him, although not her dog or even remotely important to her, Stefan seemed much older, and strangely dangerous.

Being older meant grown-up problems, Hope surmised. She wasn't sure if she wanted to be young adult-ish right now, as Stefan believed she was. Many times, in her studies about her future life as an astronaut, she had wished to be more mature, but in this moment, she preferred the safety of youth. She wasn't sure how to tell him the truth.

She didn't want to look silly or like a liar. But she also couldn't stand to keep up this foolish charade.

◢ *Nineteen* ◣

The Funeral

When Mr. Box was feeling up to it, we held a small burial for Stinky. Lined up as a funeral procession, all six of us went deep into the woods in the evening. Mr. Box carried a shovel while Abel and I pulled a wrapped-up Stinky behind us in a wagon. Aunt Esther and Alice led the way with lanterns. Hope and Stefan walked the slowest behind Abel and me.

I looked up and saw the bright full moon

sulking over us as we walked deeper and deeper into the woods. The trees surrounded us like mourners on our sorrowful journey.

We stopped when Mr. Box found a good spot where the lights from the campground were barely visible and the dirt was soft. Mr. Box drove the shovel into the stubborn ground. The earth reluctantly opened shovel by shovel, ready to receive its new friend. Mr. Box was old but strong. His arms rhythmically moved with strength and persistence as he dug deep into the ground.

Alice and Aunt Esther offered to take turns digging, but Mr. Box said he was an expert hole digger. "Been digging holes before I could walk. Farmer Judd Junkins don't let you be a tender toddler on the Salt Lick Farm that I grew up on. I was raised to work from dawn till dusk."

"Sir, would you mind letting me do that?" Stefan asked if he could take over.

"It's okay, son. I forgive you. I know you wasn't intending to run over my Stinky."

"Please, sir," the boy pleaded. There was a fluctuation in his voice that made me feel sorry for him. Mr. Box was right; the boy didn't mean to hurt Stinky. It was an accident.

Mr. Box looked up, wiped his brow, offered Stefan the shovel and with some help stepped out of the hole.

"Thank you," Stefan said as he jumped into the hole, ready to move the earth.

Even a young man like Stefan took a good while because he had to dig a hole deep and wide enough so that Stinky could rest comfortably in peace.

Mr. Box couldn't sit still so he moved the dirt away that stood near the hole. He whistled an old rustic tune that went along with each stab and flow of the shovel. Eventually the grave was ready.

"C'mon out son," Mr. Box held out his hand for Stefan to grab. He pulled the boy up then Mr. Box carefully lowered himself inside the grave.

"Bring her down to me," he said after wiping away some of the dirt that grabbed ahold of his pants.

Aunt Esther, Alice, and Stefan gently lifted the poor pup, kneeled down, then lowered her to Mr. Box's outstretched hands. He held her like a baby and sang a sweet song:

There once was a pup who had a little nose
each day she grew, she slept and she rose.
Stinky Dog, stinky dog.
She nosed through the trash and ate up all my
twinkies.
She played in the puddles and got extra stinky.
Stinky Dog, stinky dog.
But even though she stunk and was a tad bit ugly
She was my super special girl who made my life
extra snuggly.
Stinky Dog, stinky dog.

His voice cracked on the last verse. Poor Mr. Box … we all mourned for him and poor smelly Stinky. He kneeled and set her in the bottom of the hole then rearranged her so that she would be more comfortable. He dragged over some of the dirt from the top and placed it around her.

With Stefan, Aunt Esther, and Alice's help, he climbed out. Mr. Box sat on the wagon as Stefan filled in the rest. After he was finished, everyone stood solemnly. I felt the need to say something, but when I went to speak, I put my hands together, lifted them to my nose, and prayed … "Dear Lord, please take good care of Stinky and Nana. Please make sure that Stinky will be happy in the afterlife and that Mr. Box won't be too sad. And make Stinky into a puppy dog angel with glittery wings that help her fly around with all the other angels like Nana. And tell Nana that we miss her and that we love her, amen."

After I finished, I felt a hand holding mine. It was Mr. Box's. He said, "Amen," then everyone else held hands and said "Amen", too.

AMAZING GRACE NEWTON

❦ *Twenty* ❧

Nonsense

As we were on our way back to the campsite, Abel asked if dogs went to Heaven.

"Yes," I said without a doubt.

He wondered if I thought that Nana would take care of Stinky in Heaven. "Will Stinky have wings like an angel?" he asked.

"Probably," I shrugged.

"Will they be white or black?"

"Probably black like the rest of her fur

would have been if she had any."

"Do you think she will have fur in Heaven?"

"You guys sound so ridiculous," Hope said as if she could take no more of our chatter. "Seriously."

"I don't think it's ridiculous at all," Mr. Box said.

Hope looked ashamed. "I'm sorry Mr. Box, I shouldn't have said that," she offered.

"Don't be sorry, dear. I just want to know why you think it sounds ridiculous?" he asked Hope.

"Well, see, they are always having these kinds of discussions, and I guess I just think it's nonsense."

"Nonsense, huh? Well, you are right about that. The world *is* full of nonsense. You know, if you think about it, actually the universe is in fact, nonsense. Nothing really makes any kind of sense."

Hope didn't seem to know what Mr. Box was talking about, and, actually, I didn't either.

"Don't you think it's a bit strange that we as humans love? Why do we love? It's complete nonsense. There ain't no reason to love; we just do. Why on earth would I love such a smelly, sad dog like Stinky? Makes no sense but I did. I still love her." Mr. Box sniffed quietly. It got extra quiet as everyone wondered why we loved.

"Loving just makes you vulnerable to be hurt, so why on earth would anyone choose to love another being that will leave you all alone one day? … Pure nonsense." Mr. Box shook his head and looked up into the sky.

"What has always really made me wonder is, given what we know, how is it that out of all the infinite numbers of galaxies, planets, and solar systems, why would only this here Earth hold life? One out of a billion planets? And don't you think it's nonsense that we are orbiting around a suspended ball of constant burning gas at just the right distance away to not kill us? If we were any closer to the sun, we'd all burn up to a crisp or any farther, we'd freeze to death."

A shiver ran through my whole body. I looked over at Abel who was looking up at the moon as we walked. His mouth gaped open as he followed our group, for once, not running ahead.

Aunt Esther quietly spoke, "Or what about the fact that our bodies are hunks of clay made from the same minerals found in the earth? And that those bodies walk around thinking thoughts about outer space?"

We all laughed lightly, but I pictured our bodies doing exactly what they were currently doing … hunks of clay, walking around, thinking thoughts about outer space.

When we finally made it back to the campsite, Mr. Box said his goodnights. But before he turned to go, I said, "Wait, I have something for you."

"Oh?" he wondered.

"Yes. Here, this is for you." I reached into my pocket and grabbed the wad of cash and placed it in his hands.

He shook his head and said. "I'm sorry, Grace. I just can't take it. How about you and your brother and sister split it and go out for ice-cream or something. That would make me feel better."

I looked up at Aunt Esther. She nodded, and then I looked back at Mr. Box as he placed the money back into my hand.

"Yes, sir," I said.

He smiled then turned to walk home alone.

AMAZING GRACE NEWTON

↩ *Twenty-One* ↪

Forgiveness

Before Hope went to join her family for the remainder of the evening, Stefan gently tugged her arm, "Can you ever forgive me, Hope?" Stefan asked.

"It was an accident, Stefan. There is really nothing to forgive."

"Then why do I feel like I've done something wrong to you?" he searched Hope's hazel eyes for an answer.

"*You* didn't do anything wrong. It's just that I think you may have the wrong idea about me."

Stefan looked confused and a tad irritated. "I'm *so* not sure what you mean."

Hope had never intended to be untruthful to Stefan so when it came time to confess, she felt mostly … not sorry. She had mixed feelings about her predicament. If she were to confess, she wasn't sure if she would sound pathetic or like a liar—neither one was acceptable to her.

She wanted to go home and avoid the whole confrontation, but something drew her to Stefan. He was a good guy who tried very hard to make good on a horrible mistake he had made … something she had yet to do.

"We would die," Hope randomly said.

"Huh?"

"We would die," Hope repeated.

"What are you talking about?" Stefan was confused.

"Remember that dream you had? When you said that your car became a rocket and we were floating around in outer space with no protective gear on?"

Stefan gave Hope a strange look. "*Uhhm*, yeah, I remember."

"Well, we couldn't survive by kissing. We would suffocate or die of carbon dioxide poisoning," Hope said nervously, pacing back and forth.

Stefan gave her a strange look. "Yes, you are right, but it was just a dream. Are you okay?"

"I'm sorry Stefan, I can't keep doing this."

"Doing what?" he searched her darting eyes for an answer.

"Just … Just … Never mind."

AMAZING GRACE NEWTON

⋰ *Twenty-Two* ⋱
Puddles

I went to sleep with tears forming in my ducts. I was thinking about poor Stinky's face when she had died. It was the only moment in her whole life that she wasn't picking at herself or crying out in self-made agony.

I pictured Nana holding Stinky the way Mr. Box had. Nana would take good care of Stinky. That thought must have finally put me to sleep.

My dreams drifted around like a rowboat stopping in different puddles to drop into. In the last puddle, I found Mazie swimming around like a mermaid. She looked so pretty with her long strawberry-blonde hair, her turquoise tail, and shell top. She was going along the bottom of the ocean floor over coral reef. She was peeking inside the tall grasses, teasing the fish inside. I swam up to her, wanting to let her know that I was here. When I got close to her, there was a wall of clear glass between us. She saw me and we waved at each other. We swam up face to face. I pounded on the glass at the same time she did. My face must have looked confused because her expression matched mine. Everything I did after that, she did exactly the same. She must have been playing with me … silly Mazie.

I jerked awake even though the sun wasn't quite out. I looked at the grey sky in between blinking. After I woke and had breakfast, I headed on over to see Mr. Box.

The air felt fresh and cool. A fog floated along, swam through the bushes and into the distance. I walked slowly, listening to the silence. For once I didn't hear Nelson being yelled at for something.

I knocked on Mr. Box's camper door, but he didn't answer. That was strange, I thought. He was always here. Where was he? I looked around but my eyes landed on his carvings. I got lost in the details. His artwork was amazing. I could stare at the pieces all day long and still not see every one of his feathery strokes.

"Well, who do we have here, so fresh and early this morning?" Mr. Box asked from behind me. I turned to see him holding a heavy log in his hands.

"What's that?" I asked about the log.

"She going to be Stinky," he said as he set it down and patted it.

"That sounds funny," I chuckled.

"That's why I named her that."

"I thought you said it was because she was stinky?"

"Actually she didn't stink when I had named her." He chuckled then said, "I just thought it was funny."

"Oh," I said while scrunching my face.

"Yup, there's a lot to a name," he said.

"You said that before."

"I know and I'll probably say it again.

"What does it mean?"

"Well, in order for you to understand, I have to tell you a long story."

After he said that sentence he didn't say anything else for a while.

"Are you going to tell me or what?" I asked.

"Most people don't have time for long stories."

I thought about all the things I could be doing with my time then answered, "I do."

"Well, all right then … pull up a chair and get comfy while I get out my widdlin' tools."

ᥱᥣ *Twenty-Three* ᥱᥣ

Widdlin'

I ran back to my camp and grabbed one of our extra folding chairs, struggling to bring it back while Mr. Box was all set to make a Stinky dog carving.

After I sat down, he handed me a little stick and a knife to do my own widdlin'. "Make sure you always push the knife away from you, ya hear?"

"Yes, sir," I answered.

"Sir," he chuckled. "Now that's a name I was close to never being called."

"What do you mean?"

"Well, let's just say, when you were never meant to be nothin' and people treat you like a nothin', they don't refer to you as a sir. I was called Box Boy till I was eighteen years old."

"Box Boy? Why?"

"Long, long time ago, when men were made of iron and boats were made of wood, I was delivered. Most people are born, I know, but I was boxed and brought to a farm and left there."

"You were born in a box?"

"Either that or somebody put me there soon after. I don't know if it was my momma or daddy who gave me away. All's I know is one day, I showed up in a box on Farmer Judd Junkins' farm. He found me out near the barn close to the road. Saw a little baby and thought about leaving me there but instead carried me in ... was the only grace I received from him during my time on The Salt Lick Farm."

He paused a minute before continuing.

"Never knew my real parents, but I didn't forget from where I came because Farmer Judd Junkins never failed to remind me every single day that I was no son of his and that I came from a box. That's why they called me Box Boy. Worked long hours every day. Got the tough skin and color to prove it. It's as thick as it is brown … browner than most other colored folks, I reckon. Actually, I never understood the term colored. Far as I could see, we're all colored. Even you got a color, it's kind of a creamy yellow ochre, burnt sienna combination with speckles … Still, to this day, never saw a clear person."

"Me neither," I imagined what a clear person might look like … *probably like a bubble.*

"Farmer Junkins had two *real* sons and three daughters. They all got to sleep indoors. I slept with the animals in the barn. Those horses, cows, goats, and chickens were my *real* family. Most of the Junkins kids paid me no mind except for the youngest daughter, Elise. She was my friend. In fact, you remind me of her, a lot."

That made me smile. I glanced down at

my wood that I was close to butchering then looked over at Mr. Box's log. It didn't resemble anything yet, but it still was better than mine.

"Is that how you learned to carve all these animals? Because you lived with them?" I asked.

"You sure are a sharp youngin'," he chuckled. "You could say so."

"What was Elise like?"

"Well, she was nice."

"No, I mean what did she look like?"

"Well, now… let's see …" He turned away from his log. He closed his milky eyes then peered up toward the sky. "Back then, when she was a little girl, she had bright sparkly eyes that looked like green marbles with brilliant stars for pupils. Let's see … her skin matched the hay in the barn and her hair was a short brown bob … like I said, cute, like you."

I smiled again.

"Every night, she snuck some dinner over to me in the barn, warm blankets, and lots of books."

"Books?" I said with an upside down face.

"Yeah, what's wrong with books?"

"They have words in them and uh …

they're boring."

"They're only boring if you don't know how to read," he said casually. But then he looked up. "Now wait, do you know how to read?"

"Yes!" I lied. But he looked at me with a skeptical eye. "No," I admitted.

"No?"

"It's just that I can't seem to remember what sounds the letters make and stuff … finish telling me about your name." I changed the subject.

"But," he started to say before I interrupted.

"I thought you said it was a long story and I want to hear it all," I pleaded.

His eyes made the same skeptical movement from before but then softened when he went back to his story.

AMAZING GRACE NEWTON

❧ *Twenty-Four* ❧
The Name Game

"You want to hear about my name, now do ya? Well, all right then. Like I said, I was called Box Boy until one day, after all the kids was grown up. Elise was about to go away to secretarial school and I didn't want to be stuck on the farm with Farmer Junkins, alone, with no one to bring me dinner, blankets, or books. I told her that I wanted to go sign up for the Navy. I had read many school books about

American history and wanted to serve my country, plus I just had to get off The Salt Lick Farm."

"One day, Elise woke me up extra early in the morning and told me that we had to scoot right away. There was no time for goodbyes to the animals who had kept me company and warm all those years. We had to go. She had 'borrowed' her daddy's pickup so she could drive me to the Navy recruiter's office. She had to have the truck back before the farmer knew it was missing."

"Grace! Grace!" I heard Abel call in the distance. "Where are you? Oh, there you are," he said from behind me. I turned to look at Abel as he was rolling his fists around his tired little eyeballs. "You want to go to the lake with me?"

I answered back quickly, "No."

"Aw man! Why not?"

"I'm listening to a story."

"Can I listen, too?" Abel asked.

I looked up at Mr. Box who shrugged and said, "Sure".

Abel walked up and noticed the knife and

piece of wood in my hand. I could tell he wanted to take them from me. But Mr. Box gave him a piece and a very dull knife to whiddle with. He went straight to work after Mr. Box instructed him on what not to do.

"Okay, so where was I?" Mr. Box rubbed his forehead trying to find his place in the story. "Oh, I remember … Elise had dropped me off at a strip mall where the Navy recruiting office was but it was closed because it was too early in the morning."

"Did you ever see her again? Elise?" I asked.

"Don't rush the story, now … gotta be patient."

"Yes, sir …" I slumped but got back to work on my stick.

"Wasn't sure what time they opened so after a while I started walking around and saw the office down the way was the Army office. They're business hours were stated on a sign hanging on the door. It opened at 8:00 AM. I had no idea what time it was so I wasn't sure how long I would have to wait. So I kept on walking, lookin' for a clock till I got to the Marine's office and there was a white man sitting at the desk.

I looked in, but when he looked up at me, I walked on by. I kept walking to the end of the strip mall then turned around. When I was walking back, the man at the Marine's office was standing outside the open door."

"What did he say to you?" Abel asked.

"How'd you know he said anything?" Mr. Box asked.

"Just figured."

"Okay, well, you figured right. He said, 'Hello there, soldier, you looking to be somebody? Want to be a Marine?'"

"I replied, *well uh, sir, actually, I'm here to sign up with the Navy*."

"He chuckled and said, 'They're closed right?'"

"*Yeah*, I said back."

"He looked back at their closed door, looked back at me then said, 'Those lily white sea lovers are too lazy to get here on time. If you want to be a real somebody, you want to be a Marine!'"

"Did you want to be a Marine?" I asked.

"Not at first, no. I had in my head that I was going to be in the Navy and sail away, far as possible. I didn't know nothin' about the Marines. But this was where I learned my name."

"Learned your name? What do you mean?" Abel asked.

"See, another Marine showed up after a while. He was tall, he was strong, and he was what a real man looked like. I hadn't seen one of my own kind in such a commanding position. But when he walked into the room and spoke to me in such a way, asking me real questions, I then wanted to be like *him*, a Marine."

He paused for a second then said, "After the officer was done explaining what I would become when the Marine Corps was finished with me, he asked if I wanted to sign up and I said, *yes sir!*"

"He asked me my name, but he said, 'What's your name boy?'"

"I said *my name's Box Boy*."

"He told me, 'That wasn't no name'. He asked me how old I was."

"Told him I thought around seventeen."

"He asked, 'What do you mean?'"

"I told him about how I had come to be

named Box Boy, and how I had lived on Judd Junkins' Salt Lick Farm, and how I slept in the barn with the cows, goats, and horses."

"The officer was quiet for a minute, looked around the room then at the other officer who shrugged his shoulders. He lifted his hand up to his downturned forehead then asked, 'If you could have any name in the world, if you could pick any name out of all the names you have ever heard in the whole wide world, what would your name be?'"

I had never thought I could have my own name, like Elise had her own and Farmer Judd Junkins had his own name—even though *I* didn't think his name sounded all that great. So, I thought about all the books and histories I had read. I wanted to have a noble name, a name that was respected. I thought about a man who had a great name, with his name, did great things, and said great things like ... '*By failing to prepare, you are preparing to fail*'." Mr. Box paused for a moment.

"Or this is a good one ... '*We are all born ignorant but one must work hard to remain ignorant*'."

Those *were* good sayings, I thought.

"So, *I* said, *I'd like the name Benjamin Franklin*."

"Then the recruiter wrote down the name, filled in the rest of the paperwork, then said, 'Well, Happy Birthday, Benjamin Franklin Box because you're eighteen, today'."

"That was January 17, 1947. So whatever, whoever I was before, was gone. I was now Benjamin Franklin Box and it felt good to have a name."

AMAZING GRACE NEWTON

✦ Twenty-Five ✦

"Panths"

"Knock, knock," Mr. Morsel said in a silly manner as he walked up to Mr. Box's campsite.

"Who's there?" Abel and I asked.

"Panther."

"Panther, who?"

"Panther no panths, I'm goin' thwimming."

Abel and I chuckled a second, understanding the joke that got even funnier when we noticed how Mr. and Mrs. Morsel were dressed. He was holding Punky in his baby sling, who was wearing some oversized sunglasses while Mr. Morsel was dressed in high-waisted, big, pink drawstring bathing trunks, socks and sandals, a baseball cap, and a towel wrapped around his shoulders.

"You still telling that old joke?" Mr. Box shook his head.

"This old man boring you kids with his stories?" Mr. Morsel said.

I hadn't realized that Mr. Box was finished talking because I will still re-playing his last sentence in my head when Mr. and Mrs. Morsel had walked up.

"What are you planning on doing with that?" Mrs. Morsel asked me about my horrendous carving of a who-knows-what.

I shrugged.

"Well, don't hurt anyone with it. Looks sharp," Mrs. Morsel warned.

I looked at my thing that I had whittled down to a tiny spear and stuck it between my teeth.

"You kids ready for the big treasure hunt?" asked Mr. Morsel.

"Treasure hunt?" Abel and I questioned.

Mr. Morsel shook his head. "Yeah, don't they tell you anything? Sheesh, poor kids."

"Well, are you going to tell them or what, Marty?" Mrs. Morsel rolled her neck around as she gently tapped his arm.

"You want me to tell them?"

She rolled her eyes.

"Ha ha! I'm just yankin' your chains." Punky, their little baby dog, blinked while Mr. Morsel yanked our chains.

"I want to know about the treasure hunt!" I said.

"Okay, kids," he bent over and whispered in a silly way. "There's a big scavenger hunt this afternoon at the pavilion at 4:00 o'clock. All the kids will be there. There's a big prize for the winner. But don't tell anyone."

"He's being silly, you can tell whomever you wish," Mrs. Morsel said.

Abel and I jumped out of our seats and squealed in delight about the possibility of winning a big prize, even though we had no idea what the big prize was.

"How y'all doin'?" Mr. Box asked the couple.

"Better than we deserve, that's for sure," Mr. Morsel said, seriously, for a change.

"We deserve a whole lot of nothing, but it don't hurt to ask for something," Mr. Box said.

"Very true, so what have you guys been up to all morning?"

"None ya," Mr. Box said.

"What's that?" Mr. Morsel leaned in, thinking he had misunderstood Mr. Box.

"None ya business," Mr. Box laughed at himself and smiled.

"Well, okiedokie then. Kids if this old man gets too boring, just leave. He'll never even notice. He'll just keep on talking to himself."

The two old men had fun razzing each other.

"C'mon, you old coot," Mrs. Morsel said. "The sun will be down before we get to the lake, if you keep yammering on like this."

"Yes, Dear."

AND THE RV TRIP

AMAZING GRACE NEWTON

∽ *Twenty-Six* ∾

A Watched Clock Never Moves Fast Enough

"What time is it?" I asked as we were eating our late lunch.

"2:37," Alice answered.

"Poop."

"What's the matter?" she asked.

"It's not 4:00 o'clock."

"Is that your favorite hour?" Aunt Esther asked.

"Today it is!" I never knew you could have a favorite hour but today 4:00 o'clock was definitely my favorite.

"What's happening then?"

"A scavenger hunt at the pavilion!"

"Oh, I see."

"What time is it now?" Abel asked obviously as excited as I was.

"2:38."

I heard voices in the distance getting closer, then Hope walked up with Stefan.

"*NELSON*! Stop putting boogers on the table." Apparently now was the time for Nelson to get yelled at for everything. Nelson must be a real stinker to always be in such trouble, I thought.

AND THE RV TRIP

Camp Bushpea
Scavenger Hunt

---a pinecone
---an acorn
---a pebble
---a stick
---a flower petal
---something that looks like treasure
---something smooth
---something fuzzy
---two kinds of leaves
---a piece of trash

Twenty-Seven
The Hunt

After an excruciating hour and ten minutes of listening to Nelson getting yelled at next door, Alice told us that we had better head on down to the scavenger hunt if we wanted to get there on time.

When we got to the road, a boy was standing there. It was the same boy that I had seen at the caverns.

"*NELSON*! Get back here before I whip your behind."

That was Nelson? The boy from Tuckaleechee Caverns?

He looked at us then ran back to his campsite. Boy, was I shocked.

"C'mon Grace! We're going to be late!" Abel said.

"Okay!" We ran like the dickens. By the time we reached the pavilion, I was out of breath. I huffed and puffed while Abel barely suffered. He was pacing the ground ready to find his treasure.

A fine, mustached young man with the fluffiest, fullest, bounciest, bulbous blonde hair, sculpted by a visor, blew a whistle and asked everyone for their attention.

"Welcome to Camp Bushpea's seasonal scavenger hunt."

This already sounded exciting.

He explained the rules and gave us each a list of things to find. As he read the list, I drew in some picture examples to go along with the words so I would be able to remember what I was looking for. As soon as he had finished,

Abel and I took off into the woods, racing each other to find each item.

So far, I found a pinecone, an acorn, something smooth, two kinds of leaves, a stick, a piece of trash, something fuzzy, and a pebble. I looked down at my list and all I needed to find was something rough, a flower petal, and something that looked like treasure.

What could possibly look like treasure? I looked at the picture of a treasure chest. I had never seen inside a real pirate's chest but I imagined it would be overflowing with goblets of gold, silver coins, and pearl necklaces. I doubted there was a pirate's chest here at Camp Igottapoopie so something else would have to do. What would the prize be for finding all of this?

I wondered how many things Abel had found so far. Was he ahead of me? Did he find treasure? As I wondered, I looked around for Abel. Where was Abel?

AMAZING GRACE NEWTON

✍ *Twenty-Eight* ✎
Getting Real

As Stefan was playing one of his favorite songs, he performed an excellent solo rendition using the air drums. Hope was amused by his antics. Stefan was very enthusiastic about the music he liked; it showed in his every emotion. Hope had never heard of any of these songs so when he was trying to sing them (badly), she still had no idea whom he was emulating.

"You like The Warblers?" Aunt Esther said

as she was passing by. "They're from my time!"

"Your time? Personally, and no offense, but I think they're sound is timeless," Stefan perked up when he found a fellow Warbler fan.

"No offense taken. They *are* timeless," Aunt Esther agreed.

Stefan got excited especially when it came to subjects like music, cars, cars, and music. He liked sports cars with great sound systems … systems that "crystallized" music, as he termed it. Hope couldn't care less about either of the subjects and nudged Stefan to leave with her but before they left Aunt Esther called out, "Hey, wait."

They turned around.

"I'm sorry, but, you know, we've been through a lot together and all but, sadly, I never got your name," Aunt Esther said to Stefan but gave Hope a blaming stare for never introducing them.

"Oh, it's …" he began to say.

Aunt Esther was getting ready to sit down next to Alice. "C'mon over here so I can hear you better; we won't bite."

The teens walked back over to the campfire

where Aunt Esther and Alice were sitting.

"So, you were saying?" Aunt Esther asked Stefan to continue.

He cleared his throat then said, "Stefan."

"Stefan what?"

"Steele."

"Stefan Steele! That's a fascinating name. Are you a movie star or are you foreign?" Alice chuckled.

"I'm from Virginia."

Aunt Esther and Alice looked at each other and said, "Definitely foreign," then laughed again.

"You seem to know a lot about our kind of music for someone so young. How old are you?" Aunt Esther gave Stefan a thorough inspection, one that she probably should have done a couple days ago. "If I wasn't mistaken, you look to be around sixteen, close to seventeen, am I right?"

Hope began to panic. She knew where this was going, and she was not ready to do this right now.

"Yeah," Stefan nodded.

"Oh, an older boy! Hope, you little panther!"

"Only by a year," Stefan said. "Hardly noticeable, right?" He casually looked at Hope, thinking that she would agree with him.

Aunt Esther and Alice laughed heartily. "He's cute Hope but not very good at math."

Confusion washed over Stefan's features. "What are they talking about, Hope?" Stefan searched Hope's eyes for answers.

Aunt Esther and Alice suddenly became quiet when they saw the look on Hope's face. Guilt was written on it like a blinking neon sign.

"Oh, silly us. We're actually the ones who are bad at math. These kids grow up so fast, it's hard to keep track. Hope, you're what, fifteen, right?"

They tried to cover for her, but it was too late. It was obvious. Hope had to come clean before she lost her mind. This had been bugging her the second the misunderstanding had not been clarified.

"Stefan, I'm sorry, but I am only thirteen years old. I'm not fifteen as I led you to believe," Hope confessed. When all the words came out, a ginormous weight was lifted off her shoulders. The little lie was way too heavy for her to be burdened with any longer. But the look of shock that Stefan shot her left her with an entirely different feeling, and it wasn't good.

"You're what?" Stefan's disbelief looked like he had found out that Hope was really an alien.

"Thirteen."

"I know, but oh my gosh." Stefan stood dumfounded.

The Morsel's walked up, still wet from being at the lake. "Knock, knock," Mr. Morsel said.

Stefan walked away without saying a word.

Mr. Morsel watched as the boy swiftly strode away then asked, "Was it something I said?"

✄ *Twenty-Nine* ✄
Unfriendly Trees

"Abel?" I called out.

"Abel?" I called louder.

I ran around the bushes and called his name for what felt like too long. Uh-oh, I was so busy looking for all the other stuff that I lost my brother. I wandered around dashing from tree to bush hoping to find Abel crouched down looking for items on his list.

Before I knew it, I got myself lost, too.

Where was I? I looked around—nothing looked familiar. Well, actually it all—the trees and leaves, looked the same. Oh no, where was I? I started to panic. What would I do? What should I do? The warm blood that rose to my cheeks ran down to my gut making my head feel light and my stomach queasy.

Tears began to fill my eyes. Maybe I should stop and stay put. I flopped down on my butt and wrapped my arms around my legs. All of the items I had found earlier spilled onto the ground beside me.

Poop.

I put my head down and tried to breathe as panic took hold of my thoughts. I heard a noise in front of me. A sparkle vanished into a flower. What was that? I crawled over to the large open petals and found a tiny pool of water with Mazie looking back at me. My frown turned upside down.

"Mazie!"

"I found you!" she said.

"I'm so glad you found me because I'm actually lost."

"Grace you are never truly lost, for you

have been found."

"I have?"

"Yes!"

"Who found me?"

"I found you!" said someone from behind me.

I turned and practically bowled him over in excitement. "You did find me! You did! Thank you, Abel, thank you!"

But it wasn't Abel who had found me. It was Nelson.

"Oh sorry, I was just looking for my brother," I said, obviously embarrassed.

Nelson looked a little confused but also proud to have found me.

Just as things were about to get awkward, Abel ran up saying, "Grace I found all the things on the list, let's go back and get our grand prize!"

"You did?"

"Yes!"

Nelson stood quietly as Abel and I exchanged our information.

"Wow! Even some treasure?" I asked.

"Yeah, I found this nickel on the ground.

That's treasure, right?"

Funny how I made something not difficult into something so complicated. Why didn't I think to look for a coin?

"You are right! Let's go!" I said as we began to go. I looked at Nelson and asked if he wanted to come back with us.

"I still have some things to find first. I'll see you back there," the boy said as he started to go on his way.

"Okay," I said. "Thanks for finding me."

"You're welcome." He smiled before turning to go.

Nelson wasn't bad. He was good, I thought to myself.

"C'mon, Grace! Let's go!" Abel said.

We ran as quickly as possible. The sun was already setting. The crickets chirped as the woods grew darker. We ran, getting more and more out of breath, when I realized that we were running in circles.

"Wait, we've been here before, Abel. I think we need to take a different turn," I said while trying to catch my breath.

Instead of running, we walked quickly but

still found no way out. *Now, we were lost for sure. Double Poop.*

I called out, "HELP!" hoping Nelson might hear me. But no one heard my cries. Abel hollered, too. At least I wasn't alone.

I was looking down at the ground trying to find a flower so I could get some help from Mazie, but no blooms were open.

"Grace?" Abel pointed. "What's that?"

"What?"

"That mound of dirt."

"I don't know," I said. I looked around as dusk made the trees look less friendly. The poem that Aunt Esther read to me replayed in my memory and then it struck me what that mound of dirt could be. "Actually, it looks like an Indian burial mound."

"How do you know?" he asked.

"I remember finding mounds just like this with Smith and Wesson from the woods back home. They always called them Indian burial mounds. And we better not disturb it or the spirits will get us."

Abel suddenly looked scared. The whites in his eyes grew larger than I had ever seen them.

"How do you know?" he asked.

"Alice told me," I said, as if that should explain everything.

It was dark. I could barely see anything. I wanted to get away from this sacred site but was too scared to go any further.

৩ *Thirty* ৩

The Truth Will Set You Free, Right?

"Do you hate me now?" Hope asked Stefan when she found him sitting on one of the swings in the kiddie park.

After a couple of seconds, Stefan said, "Hate is not a word I choose to use often."

"Okay, then, do you dislike me?" she asked, hoping he would say no.

He breathed out quickly then said, "I do not like the fact that you misled me, but seriously, how can I not like you? I mean, I kind of really, really like you, but ..."

Even though it was getting dark, Stefan looked into her eyes. Hope could sense waves of emotions washing through his thoughts.

"Stefan, I'm sorry." She owed him an apology. "Can you ever forgive me?" she echoed his question when he had been laden with guilt after accidentally running over Stinky.

"Of course I forgive you. It's not like you killed somebody."

She couldn't help but let out a small snicker. *Poor Stinky*, she thought.

Stefan seemed to read her thoughts, "I'm telling you that dog came out of nowhere! I never even saw his shadow much less his body."

"Her," Hope corrected.

"Huh?"

"Stinky was a girl."

"Oh, really? Okay, then, *her* body ... I never saw her, at all."

He was quiet for a second before he queried, "Why is it worse to accidentally kill a girl dog? I don't know ... but it is." Stefan lowered his head in his hands.

"I'm sure that you never meant to do it … kind of like I never meant to lie to you."

"You never technically lied. Believe me, I have replayed all our conversations inside my head, and you never actually told me how old you were. I just assumed your age, and that is not your fault."

"Does it make a difference?" Hope asked. "My age?"

"It seems like a big age difference now. But really it's only three years, and my dad was older than my mom by five years. Plus, by the way you act and talk, you seem more mature than a lot of other girls that *are* my age."

Hope smiled.

The stars began to twinkle while the smiling moon shown. "It's getting late. I should be getting back."

"Actually, before we get you back, I need to show you something," Stefan said offering his hand to Hope.

"What is it?"

"You'll see … C'mon!" Hope took his hand as they walked down the lamp-lit path.

Hope had been down this path many times

on their way to the lake but never at night. Frogs croaked while crickets chirped within the bushes as the sounds of evening were proudly broadcasted along the way. What she couldn't see was the hidden show that was about to begin.

"Are we going to the lake?" she asked.

"Not quite," he teased.

"Where then?"

"We're almost there."

The sound of the waterfalls could be heard from up the path as they came to the suspension bridge. Stefan led Hope to the middle of the rickety bridge then stopped. Hope wondered if this was it … the middle of the suspension bridge.

She started to speak when he motioned for her to be quiet and to look over at the greenery draped walls. At first she thought the flickering of lights were lightning bugs, like they had back home. But these things, as well as the waterfalls that cascaded into the rushing river below, glowed in a spectrum of what appeared to be ultra-violet hues. It wasn't just the flying organisms that glowed, even the rich, varied foliage shimmered in all of its bioluminescent glory. Mushrooms, flower petals, ferns, and vines came alive in a fantastic light display. In a rhythmic hushed harmony, each light pulsed turning from bright-white neon yellow to various light and dark greens that transitioned to blues, turquoises, and others colors that have no names.

Hope was stunned by all the artistry that surrounded her. How could all this diverse natural beauty be random, she wondered. She thought back to what Mr. Box had said after Stinky's funeral. Maybe everything *was* too organized for it to be an accident? Staring in awe, Hope and Stefan stood speechless within the mesmerizing tranquility which surrounded them.

AMAZING GRACE NEWTON

Thirty-One

Shadow Man

I saw a dim light flash in the distance.

"Did you see that?" I asked.

"I'm scared, Grace." Apparently Abel had seen what I saw.

The light shone again. It was slowly getting closer as it swayed. What was it?

"It's the spirits, Grace. They're coming to get us for disturbing their grave."

The light came nearer and nearer.

I looked around for a hiding spot. Maybe if the Indian didn't see us, he wouldn't get us. "Come here, Abel, let's hide behind this tree," I whispered.

"Okay," he whined.

"Be quiet!"

"Sorry."

"Shhhhhh!" I said as I pulled him behind the wide tree trunk.

I heard footsteps. Oh no! Whoever was out there was headed straight for us. We quivered behind the tree, then the footsteps stopped. I peeked around the trunk and saw a tall shadow of what looked like a man holding a cross in one hand and a lantern in the other. He stuck the cross into the ground then banged it into the earth with a hammer. What was going on?

Then I heard a familiar voice singing about his Stinky dog.

"Mr. Box!" I exclaimed. "It's you!"

He casually turned around and said. "Well, hello there, Grace and Abel. What are y'all doing out here in the dark all alone? Were you coming to say something to Stinky?"

"Oh, um," I didn't know what to say.

"That warms my heart to think my Stinky dog meant so much to y'all, but she's in a better place now. She's flying with the angels like you said, Grace."

"Yeah," I said picturing Stinky flying. Even in my imagination, it looked funny for an ugly, stinky dog to be flying around with black wings.

"Your Auntie and Alice is probably worried sick about y'all. They know you're out here all alone?"

"No, we got lost during the scavenger hunt. We tried to find our way back but just kept running around in circles until we finally landed here."

"We thought this was an Indian burial mound," Abel chimed in.

Mr. Box smiled and shook his head. "I see. Well, we best get you back home before they send out an A.P.B. for you two."

"Yes sir," we said.

"Follow me," he said while signaling with his hand.

As we walked, I asked how Beverly, the RV, got her name.

AMAZING GRACE NEWTON

☙ *Thirty-Two* ❧

The Search Party

Hope said thank you to Stefan when they arrived back at camp. "Guess I'll see you tomorrow?"

"Hug?" Stefan held out his arms.

Hope put herself inside his arms.

"Kiss?" he asked while offering his cheek.

She lifted up her heels and gave him a happy peck.

"Night!"

"Night …"

Hope carefully opened the camper door. Aunt Esther and Alice where playing cards.

"How was the scavenger hunt?" Alice asked without looking up from her cards. This must have been a serious game.

"I don't know," Hope said. "Where are Grace and Abel?"

Suddenly Alice and Aunt Esther dropped their cards and looked at Hope.

"They're not with you?" Aunt Esther asked.

"No."

"What time is it?"

Hope looked at her watch. "Almost 9:00 o'clock."

"That scavenger hunt should have been over a long time ago," Aunt Esther said.

"You're right. Let's go see if we can find them." Alice stood.

"One of us should stay back here in case they come back," Hope said.

"Yes, Esther you stay here."

"No way, they're my niece and nephew; I will go look for them myself. You stay here, Alice. Hope and I will find them."

When Hope and Aunt Esther stepped outside, they came up with a plan.

"How about we split up and meet back here in one hour. If we haven't found them by then, we will call the police," Aunt Esther said with panic beginning to form in her throat.

"Okay, I'll go to the pavilion, and you go that way," Hope said while pointing her fingers.

⤸ Thirty-Three ⤷

Beverly

"Beverly? Well now, that is a wild tale. Oh, Beverly, she's been so good to me. Hmmmm … Let's see here, so way back when I was in the Marines, I met a girl …"

"Was her name Beverly?" Abel asked.

"Now, a good story can't be rushed, Abel. But to answer your question, the correct response would be no. Her name was Marsha, and she was a beaut. She had long raven-black hair, eyes to match, and her skin was smooth and soft as butter. It was love at first sight … well, when *I* first saw her, that is. She didn't notice me for a while, it seemed. She worked in the only restaurant close enough to our base that I could walk to. I used to find reasons to try to go in there like to eat or what not, but she never seemed to notice me. When I finally got the nerve to ask her on a date, she asked me what took so long."

Mr. Box laughed then looked down at us briefly before continuing his story. "We dated about a month and a half before I was sent away on assignment. Best forty-five days of my life."

He was quiet while we marched on toward the lighted lamppost that shown through the trees ahead of us, which left me wondering where the whole Beverly part came into his story.

"Um …" Abel began then tugged on my arm. I looked over at him, and he gestured that he was confused.

"You're probably wondering where I'm going with this story, right?"

"Yes, sir," said Abel.

"Uh-huh," I said.

"Beverly was Marsha's last name. Marsha had told me so much about herself and how if she was to ever have a baby girl, she would name her Beverly, for her family."

We were still confused. "So you never saw Marsha ever again?"

"Actually, I did. Many years later after I was finished with my tour, I set out to find her. Took me months to track her down. I was going to ask her to marry me. But after so many years of me being away, when I did find her again, she was already married to someone else. She even had some kids of her own, none of which were named Beverly. I guess her husband had a say in the baby naming, and Beverly was not his top choice or second or third. So when I found my camper, I named her Beverly for Marsha."

"That was nice," I said.

"Plus, she just looked like a Beverly, wouldn't you agree?"

"Yes, Ol' Tex looks like an Ol' Tex, too, doesn't he?" Abel said.

"He definitely looks like an Ol' Tex," Mr. Box agreed.

AMAZING GRACE NEWTON

✑ *Thirty-Four* ✑
But Now I'm Found

After what felt like hours, we made it to one of the main roads and headed toward our campsite. As we got closer, I could see someone running toward us. It was Hope running up to us, nearly out of breath.

"Where have you two been? We've been looking everywhere for you!"

Aunt Esther and Alice walked up with concerned faces that became relieved.

"Mr. Box! Thank you so much for finding them!" Aunt Esther said. "We were just about to call the police! We've been searching for them for the last hour."

"Yes, thank you!" Alice said while running her fingers through her frazzled hair.

Mr. Box chuckled. "They actually found me. I was just going to visit Stinky, and there they were."

"Why were you all the way over there?" Hope asked.

"Well," I began.

"We got lost," Abel finished.

"During the scavenger hunt?" Hope asked.

"Yes, first I lost Abel, then Nelson found me and then when I found Abel, we were both lost. But Abel found all of the things on the list," I explained.

"But it's too late now," Abel said forlornly.

"You're right; it is late and we will be leaving tomorrow so we better get to bed," Aunt Esther announced.

"Leaving, already?" Abel and I moaned. "But it's too soon!" we protested.

I looked over at Hope who also looked

sad about leaving. She probably didn't want to leave her boyfriend.

We said good night to Mr. Box then shuffled up into our cozy RV, Ol' Tex. After Abel and I had a quick bite to eat to fill our groaning empty bellies, we climbed up to our bunk and both looked out of the window. After a while Abel fell asleep, but my mind was still thinking. It was thinking about Mr. Box; he was such a nice man.

As if he could read my thoughts, I saw Mr. Box shooing away some naughty raccoons. Here he was taking care of us, making sure we were safe, and we had only met a few days ago.

There were so many people we knew from home, even relatives I had known forever, who wouldn't care enough to do what he had done for us in the short time that we had known one another. I wanted to do something for him before we left. I had to let him know that we appreciated him. There was only one problem … I didn't know what I could make for Mr. Box. I didn't have a sewing machine like I had used when I made all those things for my family the night of Nana's dance: Momma's dancing dress, Papa's football jersey, Hope's spacesuit, Abel's superhero cape, and the pillow in the shape of an RV for Aunt Esther and Alice.

As I drifted off to sleep, thoughts of what I could do for Mr. Box floated in and out until I zonked. I slept long and hard. I must have been extra tired from whittling sticks, the scavenger hunt, and getting lost. While I was out, I dreamed up an idea and knew exactly what I wanted to do. But I needed more than a morning to make it. I leapt from my loft and told Aunt Esther and Alice my idea.

"So can we stay one more day so I can get it done?"

"What do you say?" Alice asked Aunt Esther.

"I guess we can spare a day," Aunt Esther said.

"Yay!" I jumped up from the table and shook Abel awake.

"Huh?" His sleepy eyes fluttered.

"Abel, do you still have all the stuff from your scavenger hunt?"

"Mostly," he groggily said.

"Okay good, we just need to find one more thing," I said.

With his eyes still shut, he asked, "What?"

"A sign."

One of his bloodshot eyes opened, "From heaven?"

I laughed but then said, "No, we need to find something that we can make a sign on."

"Oh," Abel said.

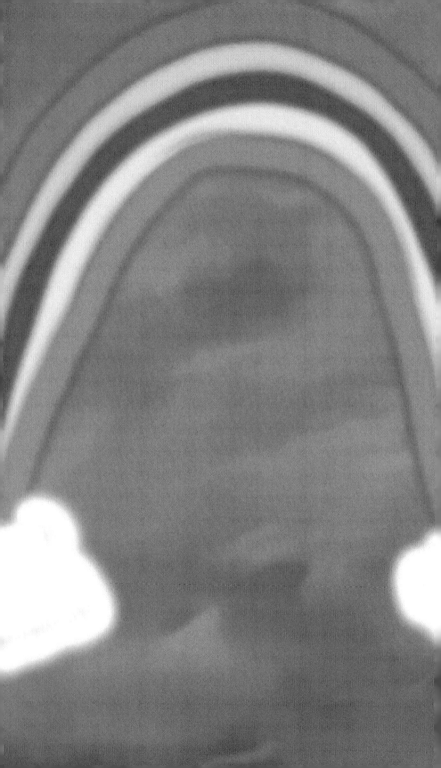

❧ Thirty-Five ❧
Looking For A Sign

Abel and I looked around but nothing really seemed perfect enough for the sign that I had in mind to make for Mr. Box. I wanted something that was like nothing else. I wanted it to be one of a kind, like Mr. Box and the star that I had knitted with the moon maiden. I walked around poking my head here and there while Abel ran to something that looked like it might have potential. He held it up and said,

"What about this, Grace?"

I said, "Nah, that's too small."

"How about this?" Abel struggled to hold what looked like a rusty old car door.

"Ha! No, that's too big."

Before I knew it, we had walked all the way to the lake. I didn't even skip a beat as we traveled across the suspension bridge or flinch as we walked through the bat tunnel. As we stood by the shore, Abel looked over the edge and found a large wooden plank that looked like it could be just the right size. It had a lot of little indentations and marks etched into its surface from being in the water for so long. I brushed off some of the filth; I could see beneath the dirt. It was perfect!

Abel and I were dragging it back to our campsite when we ran into Mr. and Mrs. Morsel.

"Knock, knock…" Mr. Morsel said.

"Who's there?" Abel and I responded.

"Atch."

"Atch who??"

"God Bless You!"

"Ha ha," Abel and I pretended to laugh.

"Where are you two headed with that hunk of junk?"

"Junk? It's not junk!" Abel scoffed.

"Oh, pardon me!" Mr. Morsel said. "That actually reminds me of another joke. It goes like this … So, there was this usher in church and a very attractive lady came in and sat in a reserved spot …"

I wanted to hurry this along because I was excited about our project, but I knew it would be rude to cut off Mr. Morsel before he was finished telling his joke.

"So …" he continued.

Abel didn't care as much about being rude and ran off. I then had to interrupt and said, "Sorry, gotta go!"

When we finally made it back to camp, Abel and I got right to work. I cleaned off the gunk with a damp rag then hosed it until the wood came clean. After letting the sunshine dry it, and a practice arrangement with the scavenger hunt items, I realized that I would need some glue so that they would stay.

"Aunt Esther, do you have any wood glue?"

"You know, I forgot to put that on my list

for camping, Grace."

"Poop."

"You know who probably does?"

"Who?"

"Mr. Box. With all those wood pieces, I'm sure he has it."

"Oh, good idea!"

I scuttled over to Mr. Box's camp and found him whittling away.

"Hi! Mr. Box."

"Good morning, Grace."

"Do you have some wood glue I can borrow?"

"What do you need it for?"

I didn't want to ruin the surprise, but I also didn't want to tell him a lie. I couldn't think of what to say. Apparently Mr. Box could see my struggle.

"Hey, if you need it. I got it, no explanation necessary. I was just bein' nosey." Mr. Box stood then rummaged through his big, handmade tool chest revealing a bright orange-topped white bottle of wood glue. "Here ya go!" he said with a smile.

I took it, smiled, then ran back to my

project. Abel was standing over it with all his goodies from the scavenger hunt.

I started to see how it would look after doing some arranging. Abel contributed to the project by accidentally farting when he crouched down. "Whoops!" he said.

We giggled at his gas blast.

Back to work, I placed the items where they were to go while Abel tried very hard to be careful with the gluing part. Needless to say, Abel got glue everywhere, including where it was necessary.

"That looks nice!" Hope said from behind us. I looked up into her face and saw a smile.

"Thanks!" Hope didn't compliment me much so I had to take note of this special occasion.

"Do you think he'll like it?"

"Of course he will," Abel said as if my question was ridiculous.

"Yes, I'm sure of it," Hope agreed.

"Lunch is ready," Alice announced.

"It's already lunchtime?" I asked, thinking that time had flown by. I wasn't even that hungry, but since we had to wait for the glue to dry, I went to eat.

When I sat down to my diagonally cut peanut butter and jelly, I looked around to make sure that I would never forget this trip. The picnic table with its red and white checkered cloth, the string of lights that dangled across to the pole with the spigot attached, the tall green trees that separated each site and the deepness of the woods just a few feet away became a lifetime memory I hoped to revisit often. "I sure am going to miss this place."

Aunt Esther and Alice smiled.

"Thank you for bringing us RVing with you," I said as I took a big bite of my sandwich.

"Yeah, this was the best trip ever!" Abel agreed.

"I couldn't agree more," Hope said, licking off a bit of jelly on her lip.

"You kids have made this trip our best yet. So thank you!" Aunt Esther said.

"I'll second that … *but* it could have been better," Alice said.

I stopped chewing because she had a serious expression on her face. Were we in trouble? I guess getting lost wasn't the smartest thing for Abel and I to do.

"How?" Aunt Esther asked befuddled.

"It could have been better if we had some ice cream," Alice said while holding a straight face. Meanwhile all of our faces brightened as we registered her folly.

"I have an even better idea!" Aunt Esther said.

"What is it?" we all asked at once.

"I'll be back," Aunt Esther said as she went inside to grab her purse.

"Grace, care to come along?"

"You betcha!"

AMAZING GRACE NEWTON

❧ *Thirty-Six* ❧
Fancy Meeting You

Hope had been casually walking around the campground, pretending not to want to see somebody. At the empty pavilion, she unnecessarily re-tied her sneakers because the laces were "too loose". After getting the tightness just right, she wandered along.

Even with all the breath-taking beauty, walking across the suspension bridge alone seemed dull.

Near the concession stand, she stood watching as a couple of kids splashed one another. A buzzing overhead called her gaze upward. The sky was clear except for an airplane that was crossing over. Intending to go to all the familiar places, she hadn't *run* into Stefan in what seemed like forever … at least fourteen hours, if not more.

A strange feeling crept over her. She was going to miss him. The sensation started to hurt her gut as she replayed Mr. Box's words about love the night of Stinky's funeral. What scientific reason was there for emotions?

She preferred the safety in physics, logic, mathematics, numbers … stuff like that. Being vulnerable for no scientific reason made no sense. In other words … nonsense.

She was getting nothing accomplished thinking about nonsense so she redirected her steps back to her campsite.

As she was almost back, she heard her name.

"Hope!"

Hope turned around.

"I've been looking all over for you," Stefan

exclaimed while holding a bundle of something.

"What do you have there?" she asked.

"It's a surprise!" he said, with his eyes rounder than the profile of the Earth.

AMAZING GRACE NEWTON

⚬ *Thirty-Seven* ⚬
Gettin' Goodies

Aunt Esther and I pedaled out of the campground, down the road to a jiffy market. She grabbed a basket and filled it with all sorts of chocolates and sweet treats. When she was finished, we were loaded with bags of happiness. It was tough, but we managed to get all of our goodies back to camp.

"Okay, Grace, I need you and Abel to distract Mr. Box for a bit while Alice and I get everything ready.

"What should we do?" I asked.

"You'll think of something, but you can't bring him back until we are ready, okay?"

"Okay," I said. "C'mon, Abel, let's go."

We walked over to Mr. Box's site and found him beginning to stand up. Since he was older, he took a while to stand.

"Hi, Mr. Box!" we said, a little overly cheerful.

"Hello, Grace, Abel, what can I do for you?"

Mr. Box was always so nice … so willing to help.

"Actually, we were wondering if you could take us for a walk so we won't get lost, again?"

"A walk? Well, uh …" He looked around at the chores, that in his mind needed to be done, then said, "You know a walk sounds like a great idea. I need to stretch my raggedy old bones anyway."

"Yay!"

Our plan worked.

Mr. Box walked slowly with me as Abel ran ahead zooming around trees, light poles, and bushes. With a cape always flying behind him,

Abel couldn't simply walk. He had to zoom.

I couldn't think of much to say because all I could imagine was the surprise that was in store.

"I bet you must be ready to see your parents," Mr. Box said.

"Huh?" I asked.

"Must been a while now, right? A week or so?"

I wasn't following his questions.

"Since you seen your parents, right? You must be excited about seeing them soon," he suggested.

"Yeah, I guess," I said, still imagining the scene we would encounter when this walk was over.

"What are you grinning about, Grace?" he asked, clearly perplexed at my expression.

"Oh, uh …" I could hardly wait. I hated secrets, but I loved surprises! However, I wasn't a very good deceiver. "You'll see," is all I could think to say.

"Oh," Mr. Box said with his brows drawing together.

↶ *Thirty-Eight* ↷
Party Time!

"Are you guys ready to go?" Aunt Esther met Mr. Box, Abel, and I on the road as we were walking up.

"Yes!!!" Abel and I jumped around like popping corn.

Mr. Box looked confused. "Come with me, Mr. Box." Aunt Esther held out her hand.

We followed, jumping up and down, excited for what we were about to see. When we entered Mr. Box's campsite, it was almost unrecognizable. Alice, Aunt Esther, and Hope had redecorated everything. They had hung all of our lights, decorations, and paper ribbons from here to there. It looked magical. At the center of his campsite stood Stefan and Hope. Stefan was holding something in a blanket that moved.

"Mr. Box, I wasn't able to sleep until I knew I could make up for what I had done." Stefan unveiled the cutest little puppy I had ever laid my eyes upon.

Mr. Box gasped.

"She's no Stinky, but this little scoop of cuteness is yours now." Stefan placed the puppy in Mr. Box's trembling hands.

Mr. Box's milky eyes welled up with tears as he fell in love with his new puppy. The tiny pup licked his face from top to bottom as Mr. Box laughed.

"Hey there, little one," he gently said while staring at his new friend.

My eyes became all watery watching Mr. Box happily loving on his new pet.

"Where did you find her?" Mr. Box asked.

"Knock, knock," Mr. Morsel said from behind us.

We all turned to see him, Mrs. Morsel, and Punky in her baby harness. Punky yelped.

We were all a bit surprised … all except for Stefan and The Morsels.

"This is Punky's sister, she needed a forever home."

"Well, she found one," Mr. Box chuckled.

"You know what this calls for?" Aunt Esther said.

"What?" most everyone replied.

"I scream, you scream, we all scream for ice cream!"

"Ice cream!" we screamed.

On the picnic table, Aunt Esther had laid out different flavors with all the fixings that we had purchased at the jiffy market. We took turns assembling our sundaes and then slurped ice cream and goodness as the stars twinkled above.

AMAZING GRACE NEWTON

∽ *Thirty-Nine* ∾
Signs of Sadness

After the ice-cream party was over, Hope and Stefan stayed later to help clean up after everyone else had left. Mr. Box and his new dog, Scoops, were getting to know one another. It was obvious that they were meant to be together. Scoops craved his attention, and Mr. Box had a lot to give.

After they were finished, Stefan walked Hope next door. Ol' Tex's campsite was almost empty. Aunt Esther and Alice had used most of their decorations for the ice-cream party next door.

"This makes me sad," Hope said.

"What?" Stefan asked.

"Seeing all the decorations down means that we'll be leaving tomorrow, and I am not ready to leave."

"I'm not ready for you to leave either," Stefan agreed as he pulled her into his arms. "Where's home?"

"Apple Valley, North Carolina."

"Nuh-uh!"

"Yes-huh," Hope said, squinting and realizing that she sounded a lot like Grace and Abel.

"That's next door to where my mom lives!"

"Nuh-uh!"

"Yes-huh!"

"Where does your mom live?"

"She lives near Asheville."

"That *is* next door!"

"So when I come to see my mom, I can come to see you. I'll have my driver's license by then."

"You hope so," Hope teased.

"What's that supposed to mean?"

"Well, just … make sure you don't hit any more little critters."

"Really?" Stefan raised his eyebrow. "Will you never let me forget that?"

"You should never want to forget that." Hope said. "Remembering what you do wrong, ensures that you won't repeat mistakes."

Stefan huffed, "Are you sure you are only thirteen?"

Hope smiled. "Yes, I'm sure."

"I have a hard time believing you."

"Why, have I lied?"

Stefan gave her a look that made her feel guilt, but it produced a smile. "I'm just a skeptic, I guess …" he said.

"Don't you forget me," Hope said seriously.

"Don't worry, you've taught me a valuable lesson about what not to forget." He smiled while looking into her eyes. "Hope, even if I wanted, I could never forget you."

AMAZING GRACE NEWTON

∞ *Forty* ∞
The Last Night

I yawned like a lazy lion. All that sugar came crashing down on my eyelids. Abel must have had the same problem because he was already sleeping face down on the booth bench below. Alice hoisted his body up into the bunk across from me. I turned to face the window and watched as Aunt Esther and Alice tidied up the campsite. Hope walked up with a smile still smeared across her lips. What was she smiling about? She flounced around, then opened the camper door.

"Hi, Hope," I said sleepily.

"Hi, Grace."

"I wish we didn't have to leave," I said as I rolled my fists around my drying eyes. "I don't want this to end."

"It's okay; it's just the beginning of a new adventure."

"Oh," I said, never thinking about it from that point of view. That was the last thought that ran through my head as I dropped into sleep. I say dropped because I felt like I was falling when my body jerked.

Five seconds later, I was out.

When morning came, I was the first to awaken. That was out of the ordinary. I never woke first. I was always last. I looked around, watching the snoring heads snuggled into their blankets. Everyone looked so peaceful. Out of the window, a fog was lifting from the ground. It was so quiet … except for the snoring.

I kind of wanted everyone to wake up, but then that would mean that we would be leaving sooner, so I climbed down as quietly as possible.

I tiptoed to the door and quietly unlocked it. A tiny squeak let out as I opened the door. I silently shushed it as I closed the latch.

Outside, the air was crisp. I breathed in the fresh Igottapoopie air. Even though it was technically called Camp Bushpea, it would be forever known as Camp Igottapoopie to us.

I heard a whining next door. I walked over to investigate then I saw Mr. Box walking his little puppy, Scoops.

Scoops was so cute! I had to go cuddle her. "Hi Scoops!"

"Well, hello, Grace. You're up early."

I nodded and siad, "Yeah," as I kneeled down to get some puppy love. Scoops jumped while sniffing my ears and licking my cheeks. It tickled. I couldn't help but giggle.

"Did you have something to do with that sign over there?" Mr. Box asked.

I looked over to where he was pointing and saw the sign that Abel and I had made, hanging nicely from Beverly's side. I had almost forgotten about that! With the new puppy and all the ice-cream …

"Abel and I did that. Do you like it?"

"I've never liked something so much," he replied.

I looked at the sign that read, "Home Sweet Beverly".

It was a good sign. Scoops wiggled over to me looking for some more fun. I sat down with my legs crossed as we played. I loved her little pink paws; they smelled like sweet corn.

From behind me, I heard a voice. "It's time, Grace. I told your parents I would have you home yesterday. I'd say we're a little late." I turned to see Aunt Esther, Alice, Hope, and Abel ready to go.

"Okay," I said, not wanting to leave.

"Goodbye, Mr. Box, it was a real pleasure being your neighbor," Aunt Esther said while giving him a hug. She kneeled down to give Scoops a tickle on her head.

"Ah," Mr. Box said, "I have to say, the pleasure was indeed all mine."

"You truly are one of a kind, Mr. Box," Alice said who also exchanged a hug with the old man.

"That's Benjamin Franklin Box, a real superhero," said Abel while saluting him. We all laughed but knew in our hearts that Abel was right. Mr. Box *was* a real superhero. He was brave enough to serve our country, tough enough to kick a bear out from our yard, thoughtful enough to bring Abel and me out of the woods safely when we were lost, and he filled our hearts with a bunch of nonsense called love.

"Super Abel, I want to thank you for such a super sign for me and my Beverly. You did good." Mr. Box ruffled Abel's dark hair. He smiled up at the old man while giving Mr. Box's long legs a good squeeze.

Hope had tears in her eyes when she said goodbye. "I hope we will get to see you again soon," she said through her emotions.

Hope's tears were contagious because when mine started, they struggled to stop.

Thanks Hope.

I guess my tears said enough because I had no words. No words were able to express how much Mr. Box meant to us. In a short period of time, he had become a lifelong friend.

I found my hand within Mr. Box's sure grip. He squeezed it before giving me a tender hug.

"We love you, Mr. Box, and I'll miss you so much," I said through muffled hiccups.

"Oh … I love y'all, too." He smiled.

"If you ever find yourself in Apple Valley, North Carolina, I'm sure these kids would love to see you. Here is my contact information." Aunt Esther gave Mr. Box an envelope which stealthily contained the money from Stefan's father.

"Oh, that would be great," Mr. Box said while wiping his own tears.

"Knock, knock." We all turned to see Mr. and Mrs. Morsel with Punky hanging in her baby harness.

"Who's there?" we said in unison.

"Looks like."

"Looks like who?"

"Looks like yer leavin'."

"Ahhhh," we said because we couldn't muster up a chuckle.

"But I'll be here all week!" *Ba da bump bump bump…* he made a sound like a drum that signaled the end of a joke.

"And then some," Mrs. Morsel said while rolling her eyes.

"We got you a little something for Scoops," Mr. Morsel said to Mr. Box.

"Oh?" Mr. Box asked.

"Yup, here you go," Mr. Morsel said as he handed Mr. Box a gift bag.

Mr. Box reached in and pulled out a special body harness for Mr. Box to carry Scoops around like a baby just like the one Mr. Morsel used for Punky.

Everyone laughed as Mr. Box tried it on.

Stefan and his father walked up behind The Morsels. "We were hoping you hadn't gone yet."

"You got here in the nick of time for one last hug goodbye," Aunt Esther said.

Instead of walking over to Hope, the boy walked over to me. "Hi, I'm Stefan. I know your leaving, but I didn't want you to leave without introducing myself."

I smiled, "Hi, I'm Grace."

He walked over to Abel who looked more skeptical when Stefan introduced himself but he complied and returned the gesture.

"Well, now that we all know each other, uh … Goodbye," Aunt Esther butted in.

"Goodbye," we all said.

⌘ *Forty-One* ⌘
Homeward Bound

Stefan and Hope gave each other one last goodbye hug before we boarded Ol' Tex.

Aunt Esther started the rumbly engine as we waved to everyone from the windows. After she pulled away from the site, Aunt Esther tooted the horn as everyone staying behind waved to us. Out of nowhere, Nelson jumped in front of everyone and waved. I wiggled my hand extra hard, hoping he'd know it was for him. I had to use my left hand to hold my waving right hand because it was getting so tired until we went around a curve that led to our long journey home, alone … Well, the five of us were alone … But not really … But it sure felt like that, especially right then.

After a while, a song by The Carpenters came on. I always liked this song. I started to hum along with the words. When the main verse came around, the whole RV was filled with song. We sang songs for hours. My voice was terrible, but I sang with a lot of gusto, and if you can't sing good, sing loud, right?

We made a couple of pit stops along the way, but when I heard the crunching of the gravel, I knew we were finally home.

It was dark as I watched the headlights light the driveway up to our house. Momma and Papa were waiting outside. They looked happy to see Ol' Tex returning filled with their family. When I saw Momma's face bubbling with joy, it made me want to cry. I couldn't wait to jump out and run into her arms.

Aunt Esther parked and shut off the RV as we kids clamored out of the door and ran straight for Momma and Papa. We were met with tons of warm hugs and sloppy kisses. Only at this moment did I realize how much I had missed my parents. Being wrapped in their arms, smelling their familiar scents, and looking into their water-colored eyes made being at home feel like the best sensation ever.

When I walked inside our warm, cozy tree-home, I sniffed up all those recognizable nutty, savory smells that made this house ours. Momma had made a big pot of creamy soup that we dipped our drop biscuits in to lap up the warm goodness. With my stomach and heart full, it sure felt great to be home.

After we cleaned up from supper, I went outside to see the moon that had been shining into the kitchen window. Its shine had followed me outside. As I stepped down from the porch, I saw a sparkle dance across the purple puddle near my special twinkling apple tree. I knew who I would see, and I ran over with excitement. When I leaned over, I saw Mazie!

"Hi! Mazie!" I was super happy to see her.

Mazie had a grin from cheek to cheek. "How was your trip?" she asked.

In the reflection, I looked up through the branches of my twinkling tree and into the shimmering sky as I recalled all the wonderful adventures we had experienced on our RV trip. I tried to think of how to describe everything while giving each moment its glory, but all I could think to say was, "It was amazing."

AND THE RV TRIP

Mrs. Goodling's
Danish Puff Recipe

1 cup flour
1 stick of butter
2 Tablespoons of water
Heat oven to 350 degrees; Mix above sort of like a pie crust. Form a ball and divide in half. Pat into two strips on a cookie sheet about 5 inches by 10 inches.
1 stick butter
1 cup of water
1 teaspoon of almond flavoring
1 cup of flour
3 eggs

In a pot mix water with butter and bring to a boil. You will need your hand mixer handy and the eggs separated into little bowls. You will need the flour already measured in the cup. When the water and butter are boiling, remove from heat and add the almond flavoring. Beat in the flour, stirring quickly to avoid lumps. When smooth, beat in one egg at a time beating well after each egg until smooth and creamy looking. Divide and spread over the crust. Bake about 60 minutes. Puff has a tendency to shrink while cooling, leaving a custardy portion in the center. Frost with confectioners' sugar icing. (2 cups confectioner's sugar, 2 tablespoons butter and milk and 1 teaspoon vanilla (adjust for consistency.)

Don't miss the next exciting adventure with:
*Amazing Grace Newton and
The Missing Noodle*!

AMAZING
GRACE NEWTON
and THE MISSING NOODLE

"Grace, it's time for bed," Momma called from the front porch.

"Yes, ma'am," I said as Mazie and I waved goodnight to one another.

"Who were you waving to?" Momma asked.

"Mazie," I said casually as I stepped inside the treehouse.

Momma shrugged then scooted me up the stairs.

I went straight to my room to say goodnight to Noodle who sometimes spent his late afternoons taking short naps on my bed, but he wasn't there. Well, it *was* much too late for a nap, I thought.

I peeked under the bed and inside the closet … no Noodle. I looked in Hope's and Abel's rooms … no Noodle. I searched in my parents' room … no Noodle.

Even though Noodle had free range of our home, he had a special cage that was kept in the mudroom. I looked inside it, but it was empty. I couldn't find Noodle anywhere.

Where was Noodle?

"Momma!!!! Noodle is missing!!!"

About the Author

N. Jane Quackenbush is a graduate of Palm Beach Atlantic University. She lives in an *Amazing* house filled with kitties and strange art in St. Augustine, FL. After a family trip to North Carolina, Ms. Quackenbush was inspired by the peaceful landscape and the wholesome nature of the area. Amazing Grace Newton personifies the overwhelming emotions such inspirational settings produce.

You can also stay in touch with N. Jane Quackenbush on Facebook.

N. Jane Quackenbush has also written the following Children's Picture Books:
The Rocket Ship Bed Trip
The Pirate Ship Bed Trip
The Afternoon Moon

Middle Grade Books:
The Children's Horrible House
Return to The Children's Horrible House
Escape from The Children's Horrible House

Amazing Grace Newton and The Purple Puddle
Amazing Grace Newton and The Missing Noodle

If you enjoyed reading *Amazing Grace Newton and The RV Trip*, please leave a review.

Made in the USA
Columbia, SC
28 January 2019